THE GRIM

a novella

MerrieOak Publishing

ABOUT THE AUTHOR

Eleanor Piper grew up in the West Country and spent much of her time on the moors and walking the coastal paths of Devon. She has always enjoyed the ancient history and mythology of the county she grew up in.

Also by Eleanor Piper

SHORT STORY COLLECTIONS
Between Stops

TAROT BOOKS
The Yes / No Tarot Oracle
The Lovers' Spread: A Tarot Guide to Relationship
    Compatibility

The Grim

Eleanor Piper

The Grim
a novella

MerrieOak Publishing

Originally published by Authors' Online 2012
Second edition published by MerrieOak Publishing 2015
Copyright © Eleanor Piper 2012
Cover art & design © Siobhan Smith 2012

A CIP catalogue record for this book
is available from the British Library

ISBN 978 0 9931600 0 4

MerrieOak Publishing
England

This book is also available in e-book format
ISBN 978 0 9931982 0 5

DEDICATION

In memory of my cat, Monster, my inspiration: an evil black and midnight cat, if ever I met one!

To Dartmoor for its myths, legends and its Beast.

To my first responders: Serena Cairns and Viv Laine, a big thank you. To Peter Holbrook for help re-formatting the cover. To Lisa and Lucy for their encouragement, patience and willingness to listen to me ramble on.

A request to the reader, please forgive my reinterpretation of The Dartmoor Beast and for rooting the creature's story amongst the folklore of the moors. I hope it will send a tingle down your spine. And perhaps, when you are out walking, you will ask yourself, 'what made that noise?' and wonder what might be dwelling in the darkest shadows under the bushes…

PRAISE FOR THE GRIM

"There is something ghastly loose on the moors! Forget The Hound of the Baskervilles; canines are so 20th Century. Eleanor Piper's THE GRIM lives up to its title and then some; it's gory and feral and moves like a house on fire. And I'm not going to tell you what The Grim itself is. You'll have to find out for yourself, and when you do, I guarantee you'll think twice before walking home through the moors after dark." Bruce G. Hallenbeck - filmmaker, and author of THE HAMMER VAMPIRE

'When sheep and cattle lie dead on the moor,
Murdered in the ink-black night,
Stray not into cavern or over dark tor,
For The Grim sets forth in the fading light.'

The Princetown Book – 1680

DARTMOOR NATIONAL PARK – PRESENT DAY

The western horizon was aflame with colour as the setting sun brought the clouds to life – first, in golden yellow, then in marigold, fading to brick-orange, and finally deepening red.

The last sliver of the sun descended below the horizon while the pale-blue sky deepened in hue towards the colours that heralded night.

The greens and purples of the moor shaded towards black, leaving the tors in stark silhouette.

To the northwest a strip of darkness fringed the landscape. Crag Tor, a forbidding cliff, stretched away above the barren scree slope. Lower down, woodland began – a mix of hawthorn, rowan, beech, and forestry pine. The forest nestled around the foot of Crag Tor like a shadowy blanket.

The rocky outcrop stood firm, a dark bastion against the last light of the day. At its base, a small patch of inky blackness was easy to miss amongst the permanent shadow of the cliff face. If you did investigate, it would reveal itself to be a small cave that vanished into the depths of the mountain. In the darkness claws scraped against rock as something headed up out of the stygian gloom to hunt in the sheltering night.

Silhouetted against the dying sunset, a head emerged from the cave. Feline, graceful, powerful. It yawned. Even to a distant observer, the fangs would be obvious. The creature was an apex predator, larger than a tiger and far more deadly. It raised its snout, scenting the night air.

Ms Smith was a fit lady in her mid-forties. Her clothes were immaculate (in Vogue business chic today, rather than Armani Couture).

She loved driving up to the moors. There she could unwind and shed the day's load of clients' demands regarding their architecture projects, as she exercised her lowchen, Patch, through the heather on the short-cut grass tourist paths of Haytor.

There were no people to spoil her silence; Patch was her only companion. It was fantastic in the autumn, when the tourists had left. In the summer, she chose other, less frequented routes and she drank in the solitude.

The small dog's lead made an impromptu belt around her waist, the metal clasp knocked reassuringly against her thigh as she walked.

She paused to look out over the landscape, taking her eyes off the view for a moment to check, briefly, that the moonlight reflected reassuringly off the chrome of this year's Mercedes, which stood alone and unblemished in the distance, in the roadside parking bay she always used.

As she enjoyed the view, her small dog

investigated a rabbit track.

Patch suddenly became alert. He stared out into the darkness.

Ms Smith noticed his tension.

'Patch, what's up boy?'

Patch kept staring into the darkness. He growled softly. It was an unfamiliar sound from the good natured pet.

'Patchouli?'

He looked uncertain, then loped back to her side and stuck close to her heel, very nervous.

'What's out there?'

She peered into the blackness and shone her torch against the grass and taller heathers.

Nothing.

Patch whined and looked up at Ms Smith. She checked the silky night. There was nothing there. She told herself not to be silly. But he was so close now he was getting under her feet.

The usually confident young dog was very definitely upset by something he was sensing. His nervousness was infectious. She scanned the darkness as she walked, looking for whatever had disquieted him. Not a fox. Maybe a badger? Were they dangerous to people? She increased her pace.

A near silent swish of grass to the left...

...Her torch revealed nothing but moorland.

Patch whined again. She looked at him. He was definitely scared – and he didn't take his eyes off whatever it was out there. But each time she shone her torch where he was looking, there was nothing to see but darkness, heather, shadows and grass.

Ms Smith increased her pace again, sure that they were being followed by … something.

She had scoffed at the unbelievable stories of a big cat roaming the moors when she had overheard them years ago in her local coffee shop, but now they tickled at her memory. There had never been any evidence! She told herself they were just stories, unsubstantiated rumour. But… were they just stories?

It must be a badger. Patch had her jumping at ghosts.

Her car was still a long way off.

She tried to keep her fear under control.

Patch nearly tripped her. She caught herself but felt the torch slip from her grasp and fall. It hit the ground and darkness triumphed, briefly, as its beam died.

She grabbed the torch and shook it as she started to jog, one eye on the path and the rest of her attention on getting the darned torch to work. It sputtered back into life, illuminating her face. Thank God! She felt movement in the air beside her, turned her face towards it. Her relief turned to terror. The night itself seemed to be attacking: she had a brief, shadowy glimpse of eyes and fangs.

'N—!' her scream was cut off short.

Patch fled whimpering. The noise of ripping flesh and crunching bone faded in the distance as he ran flat out. He didn't know where he was, or where he was going. He just needed to get away.

A battered old Land Rover, with a National Parks' Warden emblem on the side, cruised along under the grey morning sky. The back was filled with wire, fence posts, wood, tools and assorted useful rubbish.

Mabel Cooper, a naturally pretty thirty-four year old tomboy, drove expertly along the narrow twisting roads on her way to the first job of her day. Fixing that fence would likely take her most of the morning; she was looking forward to the workout.

The rising sun promised to burn off most of the cloud cover before lunch. It was going to be a lovely, warm autumn day.

Against the sunshine, the colours of her National Park Warden sweatshirt brought out the hazel in her eyes. She tapped her fingers and hummed along to the tune on the radio.

Mabel noticed Patch on the moor ahead and slowed the vehicle. Her happy mood changed instantly to one of concern and anger.

It was unusual to find lone pets on the moor. He – or she – was probably either lost or abandoned. Perhaps the owner had been taken ill while walking. However, dogs didn't usually leave their master alone if that were the case, and there was no obvious sign of another human being up here.

Mabel had to stop for the dog anyway but decided to check around for any sign of the owner at the same time. And if the owner was not there she'd need to trace them, check they were okay and, most importantly, find out whether they had a good reason for leaving a vulnerable animal up here by itself without food, shelter or protection.

Patch, bedraggled, cold, afraid and alone, sat amongst the heather, shivering. Mabel pulled up the Land Rover and jumped out to tend to the small hound. He, she noted, had an attractive white body with tawny patches on his shoulders, flanks and a jaunty one over his left ear. Most likely a show dog. He appeared to be in good condition, well looked after. Mabel felt a tug of concern for the owner.

She grabbed some bailer twine from the back and

headed over to the dog.

'Here boy! Here doggie!'

Patch looked at her, forlorn, lost. She had nearly reached him.

'Good boy. Good dog.'

Patch waged his tail and hesitantly came to her. He sniffed her outstretched hand.

'Good boy. There's a good boy.'

Patch licked her hand, obviously grateful for the company.

Mabel got down on her knees and took some trouble to make friends with him. Then she ruffled the fur around his neck. But she couldn't find a name tag.

She looked around. There was no sign of the owner. She checked his pads. He'd been running over some rough terrain but had no obvious injuries. She gently teased a few snagged sprigs of gorse and heather from his coat.

'What are you doing out here? 'Ey? Where's your Mummy, or your Daddy? 'Ey? Come on. You come along with me.'

Mabel looped the bailer twine through his collar and took him back to the Land Rover, talking as they went: 'Did someone dump you here?' At the back of her mind the thought, *people can be right bastards*, mixed with a thread of concern over where his owner might be.

She put Patch on the passenger seat and closed the door, shutting him in, then got in on the driver's side next to him. She dragged her lunchbox out of the footwell, dismantled her beef & mayo sandwich, ate the gherkins and fed the rest to Patch. He was hungry.

'You can come to work with me for now, then we'll try and find you a place to stay. 'Ey?'

She stroked his head. He curled up, laid his head on his paws, and looked at her mournfully. Mabel started the engine.

As she drove, the sun came out as promised.

The miles passed rapidly. The scenery quickly changed from open moor to sheltered moorland valleys.

The hillside was covered with woodland, which was separated from the road by an acre strip of field.

The shoulder-height, earth-filled, solid granite cavity walls on either side of the road were effectively hidden by deceptively soft-looking banks of grass and weeds, which clung to each on a shallow bank of earth. Trimmed bushes of either hawthorn, or gorse – occasionally beech – but everywhere brambles topped these attractive, but ultimately tourist unfriendly, scenic hedges. They were perfect for keeping livestock under control.

The earth-core stone hedges flanked each side of the asphalt. The lower side of the road was all fields, where the terrain opened up into 24/7 farming communities.

Mabel pulled up on the designated parking strip next to a gate. A sign beside the gate proudly indicated a well-used footpath and walking trail. At the far side of the field, the trail disappeared into the thick woodland.

She looked across to her small companion. She sensed he was worried about his owner but she wouldn't be able to start that hunt until she got back to her office base in a few hours' time.

'I have to work,' she said. 'Got to keep the tourists

safe; can't let 'em see nature "red in tooth and claw". You want to help?'

Mabel got out and grabbed a bag of tools from the back.

'You coming?'

Patch laid his head back down on the seat and whined.

'Your choice, mate. See you later.'

She shut the Land Rover door with her foot, shouldering the tool bag. She fetched a fence post from the back, slung it over her other shoulder and started towards the woodland.

On the uphill side of the forested path, sheep fencing separated the tourists, mature pines and tamed land from young trees and wild grazing. Farther along the way, one of the fence posts had been snapped through and the wire was down.

Sheep footprints peppered the gap; wool snagged on barbed wire showed where the beasts had forced their way through by weight of numbers.

Mabel set about detaching the barbed wire and sheep netting from the broken post. A claw hammer was the perfect tool to lever out the U-pins.

The new fence post lay where the old one had been; the wire and netting was securely attached to the top half of it. Mabel set about digging the old fence stump out of the ground.

She heeled in soil around the new post, bedding it in firmly. But as she worked, she became uneasy; it felt as though someone was watching her. As she finished the last round of bedding-in, she heard leaves rustle behind her. She looked up quickly.

There was nothing there.

Mabel went back to work.

A blackbird gave an alarm call and flew off. There was another rustle from off to the side. She paused, then casually stooped and picked up the claw hammer. She kept up the appearance of working, as if she was inspecting her tools, but actually she waited...

…Nothing.

She shook herself and reached for the new U-pins, about to secure the sheep netting to the bottom half of the post.

A silent footfall.

She whirled: teeth and blood-matted hair leaped at her from the side.

Mabel screamed and fell backwards as she tried to avoid the attack. She brought the hammer up to strike, but the animal just hung jiggling in mid-air.

It was a dead Cambridge lamb. The corpse was lowered slightly to reveal a chortling, ageless, wily moors-man with weathered skin. He looked to be in his late fifties, but Mabel thought he was older; probably just shy of seventy. This uncommon rake with a quirky, dark sense of humour had introduced himself when she first moved here – and initially she hadn't known what to make of him. He was possibly an ex-poacher, now unofficial gamekeeper for the local population. He knew everyone and every inch of the moor and she rapidly came to look on him as both a mentor and trusted friend.

His name was Shane and he was wearing, as usual, camouflage poachers' greens. His suppressed chuckles became full-bellied laughter.

'Jesus, Shane!' She recovered her composure. 'Lend us a hand?' she asked.

Shane shook the heavy lamb at her one last time,

dropped it, then clasped wrists with her, still chuckling, and pulled her to her feet.

'Your face!' he said laughing.

Mabel couldn't believe how spooked she was and started laughing too.

'Darned near gave me a hernia carrying that thing,' Shane confided.

'Darned near gave me a heart attack!'

Mabel looked at the wounds on the lamb. Its throat had been torn out.

'Where'd you find it?'

'Just over there,' He paused, troubled. 'I found three like that so far. I reckon some stray dogs must be having themselves some fun.'

Mabel looked at the bloody mess. She easily recognised the painted brand on the lamb's rump.

'Mr Cobbledick's going to be really pissed off,' she said.

'None too pleased, that's for sure,' Shane responded. 'He's asked me to take care of 'un. Second night in a row they've been spooked. First night of kills though.'

'How many dogs are doing the worrying?'

'I couldn't make out the tracks; the sheeps have churned up everything.' He paused and gave her a sharp look. 'I noticed your hitch-hiker.'

Mabel blinked.

'I found him on the way over. Poor little sod was abandoned.'

'So, he's a stray then...?'

Mabel understood the implication and stared back at Shane. As he tried to keep a straight face, she realised he was still teasing. They both laughed.

'That small scrap of a thing?'

Mabel's phone rang. They were still chuckling as she answered it.

'Phil? Hi!'

Phil sounded serious and quietly official.

'Who's with you?'

Haytor footpath was a hive of activity as a forensics team scoured the area. The Chief Pathologist, Dr Bernard Simpson, FRC Path, made field notes behind a weather screen, which had hastily been erected around the grisly corpse of Ms Smith. P.C. Deborah Wilkes and two bored police officers guarded the footpath area's approach to the scene.

In the distance, two other policemen chatted near the road. D.I. Philip Softly, a thirty-three-year-old local copper, had seen a few corpses in his time, all natural causes. He would not admit to his colleagues how disturbed this one had made him. Making the phone call to Mabel was a good reason not to look at the body.

Mabel knew something wasn't right; her levity vanished.

'Shane... What's wrong, Phil?'

Phil spoke calmly, but she knew him well enough to hear the disquiet in his voice.

'There's been a fatal attack here on Haytor. Looks like some kind of animal.'

Shane picked up on her reaction.

'What?' he asked.

'Someone's dead. Animal attack.'

Shane's eyes widened slightly in surprise.

They both looked at the lamb, then discounted it as coincidence.

Phil continued, 'I need you to come over and help secure the area... Bring Shane, we need a tracker, and he might have seen something.'

The two policemen broke from talking as Mabel's vehicle approached, but immediately went back to their discussion once they recognised the occupants.

At the off-road parking bay, Mabel pulled the Land Rover in next to several police and unmarked vehicles. Standing alone, a few metres further away, Ms Smith's car had a yellow tape cordon around it.

Patch perked up and barked twice, keen to get out, but Mabel grabbed the bailer twine lead and held him back as she and Shane got out. The small dog was so desperate that she relented and let the overwrought animal come with them. They headed for the footpath. Patch strained at the lead all the way, wanting to race ahead of them.

Shane and Mabel walked up the track from the road towards P.C. Wilkes, who stopped them from going any further. In the distance, Dr Simpson closed the weather screen, covering the corpse against the elements and prying eyes.

Patch whined as he pulled against the lead, desperate to get to Ms Smith.

Shane looked at the dog, troubled.

'I guess we know who he belonged to,' Shane said.

Phil came to greet them.

'Thanks for getting here so fast. We need to restrict access via the moor trails. Would you be able to sort that out?'

Mabel nodded.

'Will do.'

'Shane, can you take a look around in a minute, see

if you can spot any tracks? We've got nothing within ten yards of the victim.'

Shane assessed the terrain in one swift eagle-eyed glance, working out the best course to take in a moment.

'Rightyouare.'

Patch pulled Mabel towards the weather screen as they walked.

'You don't want to go up there,' said Phil, as he noticed the small dog pulling them ever closer to the corpse.

'I think this dog belonged to the victim.'

'Let P.C. Wilkes take him.'

Mabel handed Patch over to Deborah. The dog pined briefly, but P.C. Wilkes petted him until he calmed down. She took him back to the cars.

'You okay, Phil? You don't look so hot.'

She had seen him take death in his stride before without blinking so she was concerned about her friend's unusual disquiet.

'Her throat was torn out.' He swallowed some bile. 'It's not a pretty sight.'

Dr Simpson joined them. He indicated the forensic tent and said, 'I don't know yet, I need more evidence, but this might be someone trying to fake an animal attack. Either that or you've got a serious carnivore problem.' He let that sink in. 'Has anyone reported a big cat missing from the zoo or a private collection recently?'

Phil said he'd check into it.

'You'd better put out a public alert. Keep folks away.'

Phil agreed with the pathologist and Dr Simpson headed back to his car, done with the scene for now.

'Have either of you seen any trace of a big cat?' Phil asked.

'Nope.'

Then Mabel hesitated; Phil caught her look.

'What?' he asked.

Shane filled the gap while she tried to work out what to say.

'We've got some dead sheep over at Mr Cobbledick's. Probably worried by dogs...' He let the words trail off.

Phil continued the sentence for him, 'But you aren't sure it was dogs?'

'Couldn't rightly say.'

Phil's attention was distracted by a tourist who had managed to get to the weather screen and had opened it to look inside. Whoever he was, he had nerves of steel.

'Hey! You!' Phil's shout made everyone jump.

The 'tourist' turned to greet Phil as he pounded over. The officers, who were supposed to be on guard, looked embarrassed and raced to get to the interloper.

A Dictaphone was shoved under Phil's nose.

'Karl Fisher, South West Tribune. Who do you think did this?'

Phil angrily raised his voice to the policemen. 'This was supposed to be a secure area. Get him out of here!'

Karl was relentless.

'I'm going to need a statement.'

'You'll get one, at the proper time.' Phil glared at the man. 'And if you mess up a crime scene again, I'll arrest you. Now get!'

Karl smiled.

'I'm not leaving!' he stated.

The policemen twisted the resisting reporter's arms behind his back and forcefully walked him away.

'You can't silence the press! News is news!'

The other officials at the scene barely reacted as they went back to work.

Princetown, a small settlement in the middle of the moor, owed its continued presence to the prison and the summer tourist trade. The rest of the year it may as well have been a ghost town.

Mabel's Land Rover stood outside a pub called The Devil's Elbow. It was one of three, serving both locals and tourists alike, scratching a living in the off-season. The other two were The Prince Of Wales and the Three Feathers.

Inside, a few locals nursed their drinks. Mabel and Phil talked quietly but heatedly at the bar as they waited to be served.

The 52-inch flatscreen television, which helped encourage customers to fill the tavern on game nights, unobtrusively played local news in the background. It showed a view of the police activity on Haytor, with the forensics tent visible in the distance. Jenny Southfield, their reporter on the spot, knew this report was likely to be broadcast nationally, so her make-up was flawless, her attitude serious yet concerned, as she commented with professional, restrained excitement:

'There has been speculation about the presence of a large predator on the moor for several years, after a string of eyewitness reports by members of the public of a big cat roaming in the area. Today that presence has been confirmed.'

Mabel and Phil argued, paying no mind to the television or Jenny's breaking news story. Mabel thumped her fist on the bar.

'What? No!' she exclaimed, 'I feel really bad for that woman and her family. Just awful. But if it is a big cat, lost on the moor and hungry, to it, we're just meat on two legs. Can you really blame it? You can't just kill it for following its natural instincts!'

Phil glared at her.

'It ate someone. It dies,' he said.

Mabel picked at her beer mat.

He continued in a dangerously calm voice, 'I want you to show him around. Keep him company.'

'Make sure he doesn't get lost on the moor, you mean?'

Phil realised what she was thinking.

'Can I trust you on this, Mabel?' he asked, a dangerous edge to his voice.

She sighed, knowing she was not going to win.

'I don't see why we can't just dart the thing and stick it back in its cage!'

Phil and Mabel locked eyes; she was unwilling to capitulate just yet.

On the television Jenny's report continued:

'The police are calling in big cat specialist Baxter Cobb to help them track and kill The Dartmoor Beast.'

Mabel reacted to the name being given on television and turned to look. A recent picture of Baxter Cobb, standing in the hot African savannah, was displayed.

Phil noted her reaction.

'You know him?'

'Ah, crap,' Mabel said, a bitter taste in her mouth. 'This gets better and better.'

'I need you to help me on this.' Phil gave her a policeman's iron look.

Mabel fumed and said through gritted teeth, 'You owe me.'

Princetown's main square resembled a circus. Cars and vans were parked everywhere. A television news van, with its satellite dish and communication aerials, sat proudly on the Devil's Elbow forecourt.

A lot of the residents, and some slightly less than local West Country "lookyloos", turned up just to gawp at the excitement and to make themselves feel fully involved with something that was actually happening on their doorstep. The "I was there" factor counted for a lot amongst a grassroots community like Princetown's – and with it came decades' worth of rural gossip: "Do you remember when…?"

Hunt protestors with placards arrived both on foot and in cars. All three pubs and the many guest houses scattered immediately around Princetown were making the most of this rare off-season boost to the economy. The small town was suddenly in demand. One bright spark, an RPG modelling enthusiast, had shipped in plastic zoo figures of big cats from a Plymouth toy shop. He was now artfully adding dripping blood in red paint to their teeth, while one of his friends carefully stuck computer printed labels onto white miniature cardboard boxes. The end result was surprisingly professional. A third man sold them to anyone who wanted to buy "a commemorative token of the hunt for The Dartmoor Beast" from a table they had erected in his front garden.

Shane, Mabel and Phil watched the rabble milling around the town square. All three shared the feeling the whole mess could only end in trouble. The tourist season always arrived with its own set of problems, and they knew that the overexcited one-off nature of this event would only serve to exacerbate matters. Several groups of idiots with and without backpacks started to head out on foot, totally under-equipped for even a day trip to Dartmoor.

Mabel despaired. She stepped up on the bumper of the news van and shouted over the hubbub, but no one was listening.

'Can I have your attention please? The moors are dangerous!' Still no one cared to listen; she sighed then kept going. 'Your biggest risk is exposure! You must wear proper protective clothing!' She took a breath. 'Make sure someone knows where you are going! There are areas of sinking mud, there are old mine works, it is easy to get hurt or lost!' *Were they all total idiots?* 'Please, you must listen!'

Across the square, big cat spotters Gary and Liz, both in their late 30s, checked the kit lashed to their off-roader. They had invested in some upgrades to their top-end hi-tech detection equipment. They also had their favourite well-used canvas hide and nature-friendly camouflage gear. They loaded a few last items on to the vehicle and couldn't help but notice as a black Humvee full of top-notch hunting gear squealed into the square and slid to a stop next to the news van.

A man got out authoritatively. His name was Baxter Cobb and he was an experienced hunter who had travelled the globe in pursuit of his favourite prey: big game. He was confident in his own abilities, both as a hunter and as an alpha male. As an expert in his field, people always looked up to him and he enjoyed the attention. He was a handsome Yorkshire man who had reached his mid 30's without incident, despite working with very dangerous animals in some of the most hazardous places in the world. He had a certain magnetic charisma and a melt-your-heart smile which he gave freely to the people he liked.

He looked at the television news van and smiled to himself; this was where he should be. And he had deliberately dressed for the occasion in the very latest, stylish, "great white hunter" outfit. The television pictures would be great publicity for his new book. He unconsciously posed for the briefest moment as he assessed the scene.

Mabel groaned. Phil helped her down.

'I'm sure he's fine.'

Mabel shook her head. 'Get to know him.'

Liz tapped Gary on the arm. 'Hold up.'

He nodded. She left his side and marched towards Baxter but had to stop and wait at the curb, impatient for people and traffic to get out of the way so that she could cross.

Baxter, keen on the spotlight but with no real enthusiasm for bagging the zoo-bred pussy he'd been hired to kill, was only here for three reasons; two of which were the additional fame and money.

Baxter saw Mabel and smiled, full-beam.

'Mabel!'

He bounded over, wrapped his arms around her in a bear-hug, then grabbed her face and planted a huge kiss on her lips.

Mabel, bristling, shoved him off and slapped him hard.

'Screw you, Baxter!'

Shane and Phil stared, open-mouthed. This wasn't the relaxed, easygoing, peaceful woman they knew. Mabel stormed off and headed towards the sanctuary of her office.

Under his breath Baxter muttered, 'Oh boy.' In a moment he had recovered and turned, all pleasantries, as he extended his hand and gave Phil a warm double-grip handshake. 'D.I. Softly?'

'Call me Phil.'

Shane too extended his arm; he also got the double handshake.

'Shane Thomas, I'm your tracker. It'll be…' he chose his next word carefully, '…interesting watching you work, Mr Cobb.'

'Baxter. Baxter, to my friends.'

Shane indicated Mabel as she viciously slammed her office door behind her. The resounding crack made everyone flinch.

Shane asked mildly, 'What's up with Mabel?'

Baxter pursed his lips and frowned, wondering why she had reacted like that. Then again, he'd never understood her.

'Ancient history. We used to date... The lass didn't take it well when we broke up. I thought she'd be over it by now.'

'You've definitely got her hackles up,' Shane responded.

'She'll calm down.'

Phil and Shane were dubious. Baxter, oblivious, kept talking.

'The word is we have an escaped lion?'

Phil nodded, 'Perhaps. The animal seems to be a large, probably feline, carnivore. We're uncertain of the species.'

Baxter was about to respond, but Liz reached them. She stabbed Baxter in the chest with a finger.

'Murderer! You have no right to be here!'

Phil intervened.

'He was called in by the police, Madam. Mr Cobb has every right to be here. Now please, calm down and return to your group.'

Liz backed off slightly but was not prepared to give up until she had finished speaking her mind to Baxter.

'You should be ashamed of yourself!' It was lame, but (cursing her upbringing) it was all she could manage in front of polite company.

Baxter turned to Phil and said, 'Let's go.'

Phil gave Liz a stern look.

'Stay here, Madam.'

Baxter led the way. Phil and Shane lagged behind a little as they all headed for Mabel's office.

Liz harangued Baxter from where she was. 'You're here to gun down a noble creature! This rare animal is part of our history, our heritage! One of the big cats of Great Britain, part of our native wildlife! It should be a protected species!'

'You call an escaped lion "native wildlife"?' he called over his shoulder.

'Escaped from where!' she challenged.

The door to Mabel's office closed behind him, leaving Phil and Shane outside. Shane reached for the door handle and winked at Phil.

'Popular chap.'

Phil shrugged, unwilling to commit himself to an opinion so early in the relationship. Shane opened the door and they entered the National Park's Office.

Inside, it was a chaotic, yet organised, mess. Maps, local information books and pamphlets lined the walls. Equipment and the day-to-day stuff needed for Mabel's job was piled about the room. Her desk was relatively clear, although a large map (a smaller version of the one on the wall) was spread across it. Mabel stood at the window, arms crossed, hostile. She stared at the human chaos outside.

She barely reacted as Baxter, then Phil and Shane entered. With her back to them, Mabel indicated the mess outside with a sweeping gesture.

'We'd better put Dartmoor Rescue on alert.'

Phil nodded. Shane walked over to the small kitchen area, put the kettle on, then spooned some leaf tea (he knew Mabel's favourite mix: two parts Lapsang Soushong to one part Earl Grey) into a teapot.

Baxter watched Mabel's back. Her shoulders were rigid and her stance aggressive. He wondered what he had done wrong.

'Mabel–'

She instantly rounded on him, interrupting.

In the background the kettle boiled, so Shane unobtrusively set about making the tea while he listened. He poured the water over the leaves and let them brew for a while and then turned to watch Mabel and Baxter silently.

Phil wanted to intercede between the two, but thought better of it; instead he also waited to see what she would do.

'Shut up, Baxter!' She was so cross she could kill him. 'We may have to work together, but I don't have to like it. If we're going to get along, don't talk to me! Okay? Got it?'

Baxter couldn't understand her anger at him. He felt wounded and at a loss as to how to make things better. They used to be so close back in Africa.

'Sure thing. Whatever you want, lass.'

Phil relaxed, slightly. Shane handed him a cup of

tea.

Shane lifted the next cup in line and looked at Baxter.

'Milk?' Shane asked.

Baxter shook his head. He wasn't in the mood for a soft drink right now, but then it might help to distract him, keep his fingers busy…

'Sugar?' Shane asked.

'Thanks.' He looked at Mabel. 'But I'm sweet enough.'

Shane checked for fireworks, but Mabel ignored the barb and continued to glower out of the window. Shane handed Baxter his tea.

Baxter looked around, poking through Mabel's stuff to see if he could get a better handle on this woman. He had thought he knew her well.

Shane loaded three heaped spoonfuls of sugar into Mabel's cup and took it to her. She drank, spluttered, and gave Shane a look that clearly said, *What the hell!?* Shane gave a silent shrug in reply, *Well?* Mabel narrowed her eyes.

Shane indicated his pocket and surreptitiously pulled a book up so the title was visible – it was "Children's Guide To Cats Of The World".

'Homework,' Shane mouthed quietly.

He winked.

Mabel grinned.

Shane returned the book to his pocket.

Mabel went to the kitchen area and made herself a new cup of tea, minus the sugar.

Shane took his tea over to Baxter and drank it standing by him. He looked at the tanned Yorkshire man, trying to figure him out. But then his teasing streak took over.

'That woman out there? Native wildlife?' Shane queried.

Baxter smiled indulgently at him and enlightened him with a bit of hunters' mythology. It was clearly lunacy, but they'd need to know the type of idiots they'd be facing out there.

'Some crackpots believe we have a native species of big cat left over from the Ice Age.'

Shane and Phil both raised their eyebrows with disbelief.

Baxter, pleased with their reactions, continued. 'There are new species being discovered all the time, but to believe a large predator could go undetected for that long in a country as populated as the United Kingdom is just ludicrous.'

Phil gave an uncontrolled high-pitched snort of geekish laugher and said, 'D'ya-ah! "The Dangerous Wild Animals Act" isn't that old.' He chuckled happily.

Baxter made himself at home in the chair behind the desk.

Phil swallowed his mirth. The others didn't seem to share it. He became more serious. 'Do you have a plan? For catching the animal.'

Baxter smiled at them. 'We track it; I kill it.'

Shane spoke quietly, serious for once, 'You make it sound easy. Hunting's never easy. And this thing's killed a person now.'

Baxter yawned, supremely bored and laissez-faire about it.

'These zoo animals have no fear of humans. Sure, that makes them more dangerous, but their instincts aren't as sharp. They don't know how to work the terrain.' He paused. 'They're no real challenge.'

It was still a big cat, a killer. Phil wasn't about to waltz into a dangerous situation without the proper preparation or clothing. All his police training and instincts demanded an answer to that issue; it wasn't a small one. So he asked the question that was foremost on his mind, 'But, we must need special equipment, protective clothing?'

'Taken care of.' Baxter, full of confidence, smiled at D. I. Philip Softly. 'Being delivered this afternoon.' He switched targets and went from giving information to seeking information. 'Shane, you know the moors?'

Mabel, impatient, answered for him. 'He virtually lives on them. Born here. Raised here. Practically a wild man. Can we get on with this?'

Shane couldn't help smiling.

Baxter wasn't smiling. This was something he needed to know. 'Forgive my lack of trust but, are you good at tracking?'

'No.'

Shane's response was unexpected.

'Then–'

Shane interrupted, 'I'm bloody brilliant.'

'He is,' agreed Phil.

Mabel smiled.

'Oh.'

Shane could see Baxter needed more, and rightly so, so he continued. 'You're wondering if I can find this lion, track it to its den... if it has one.'

That was exactly what Baxter was wondering.

'I can,' Shane affirmed.

'Tracked many lions?' Baxter quizzed him, already knowing the answer.

'None at all.'

Shane's honest reply caught Baxter off guard. He

was about to respond, but Shane's mobile rang.

The town square was still a chaotic shambles of humanity – but slightly less crowded now, as the most organised thrill and adventure seekers began to head off onto the wilderness of Dartmoor.

Liz and Gary finished their final equipment check, got into their off-roader and set out for their chosen cat-watch destination.

More of the crowd started to leave the town square, taking their cues from the professionals who had already vacated the area. Those who were just here to gawp had mostly retired to the pubs to gossip about what they had seen so far and what they expected to happen next. Bets were being made about who might see, or even kill, or indeed get killed by, the big cat first.

They were in a sheltered moorland valley, where tame woodland gave way to lush pastures.

Mabel, Phil, a bored Baxter and the stoic farmer who owned the land – a sprightly, "eighty-years-young", Devonshire man – Mr Cobbledick, walked towards a gate. Shane strode ahead. When he reached it, his demeanour changed instantly. He stood there, thin-lipped, waiting. The others reached the gate.

The sight ahead was not for the faint of heart.

Baxter's interest was piqued. This was not run-of-the-mill.

About thirty dead sheep were lying where they had been slaughtered, their throats torn out. The churned-up mud and grass and the twisted bodies of the sheep, gave testament to their panic and the bloodthirsty killing frenzy of the predator that had butchered them.

Baxter was definitely focused now; he took in every detail.

Shane opened the gate, waited for them to pass through and then followed them in.

Baxter walked ahead, further into the field and looked about.

Mr Cobbledick spat on the ground.

'Stray dogs. Need to be shot, every last one of 'em.'

'You witnessed it?' asked Phil.

'Nope. Heard the sheep screaming. Came out with my gun but it was all over by then. No sign of the buggers.'

Mr Cobbledick turned to Shane. 'No point disturbing you in the middle of the night if they're already gone.'

Baxter examined the nearest corpse.

'Could be dogs,' he paused, 'more likely the work of a cat.'

Baxter pointed at the wound on the throat of the sheep he was examining: 'The death grip on the throat is typically feline.'

Phil was shocked by the carnage. 'But, this many?'

'I've seen it with tigers,' said Baxter. 'Surplus of prey. They get over-excited, go kill-crazy.'

The others joined him.

Baxter looked more closely at the large neck wound. It appeared to be a single bite.

'That can't be right...' Baxter was speaking to himself. 'Maybe..., more than one bite...?'

Shane scouted around and found a smeared, mangled paw-print. It looked more like a mushed-up giant's handprint; nearby there was a perfect hind paw-print. It was big and he didn't recognise the species.

Shane acted casually but Baxter was already heading over.

'What have you got?'

The others followed him.

Shane used his body language to herd Baxter towards the unreadable print, while he surreptitiously pulled the "Children's Guide To Cats Of The World" from his pocket and hid it in his map.

'Found a print over here, just looking for more,' admitted Shane.

As Baxter leaned over the distorted print, Shane flicked to the footprints page. Mabel, knowing Shane too well, checked where he had been looking before and spotted the clear print. She smiled.

Mr Cobbledick was just as canny as Shane and knew about his black sense of humour, especially with strangers like Baxter. He picked up on it and looked at the same place too.

Shane winked at them both and let Mabel see the book. She hid a smile. Mr Cobbledick blinked, troubled by the big cat's footprint.

Shane turned to Baxter, the expert. 'So, what type of animal is it?'

'You expect me to be able to tell from that?'

Shane consulted his 'map'.

'But, it's obviously a... a...'

The print wasn't on the chart.

Baxter's gaze became piercing.

Shane gave himself up and showed Baxter the clean print.

'Well, what about this one?' Shane asked. He indicated the book. 'It's not in here.'

Baxter laughed. 'I'm not surprised.' He examined

the print. Compared the size against his hand-span. It was big. He frowned. 'Well, it's a rear foot...' He looked at it from another angle. 'I don't know.'

A dark thought nagged at Mr Cobbledick.

'What do you mean, you don't know?' Phil demanded.

'This thing is huge! I... Possibly a new species?' Baxter hazarded.

Shane stirred the pot. 'Something that's gone undetected, something *native* perhaps?'

'No!' exclaimed Baxter. Then realised he was being played. 'People import illegally all the time. Someone found something unique, brought it back here for their collection and it escaped.'

'And started killing my sheep,' added Mr Cobbledick sourly.

'Amongst other things,' said Phil unhappily.

Mr Cobbledick sidled up to Shane and asked quietly, 'You don't think *it's* back?'

A moment passed before Shane understood; the question disturbed him. He and Mr Cobbledick stood silent for a moment.

Mabel saw their disquiet. 'What?'

'Just children's stories,' Shane replied. 'Nothing to fuss over.'

'Story or not, I still have a field of dead sheep. Who'm payin' for it? That's my worry.'

Dean Wood was beautiful by day and at night the deciduous trees looked quietly majestic. Home to a multitude of creatures and birds, it was a naturalist's paradise.

Liz' and Gary's canvas hide was so well-camouflaged that it would have been invisible by day, but now its presence was revealed by the soft light that glowed within it.

Inside, Liz looked at half a dozen monitors, checking the video feeds from the night-vision cameras they had concealed on trails and in likely places around the wood.

'Did you bring the chorizo?' Liz called out.

Unseen, outside Gary shouted back, 'I've got the whole hamper.'

Liz smiled.

Gary, a little way down the trail, headed towards the hide. He carried a wicker basket with a lid, two thermos flasks in a shoulder bag and a thick woollen blanket.

An owl startled in the trees off to the side and flew across the path inches away from him. It made Gary jump. He recovered from the shock, then peered into the trees, trying to see what had spooked the bird. There might be something there, but, then again, there might not.

He started walking again, listening to the sounds of the night. The faint crackle of fallen dry leaves reached his ears. Gary stopped and looked. But nothing was visible.

He listened for a moment. There was no more noise and nothing that he could see in the area. He breathed in through his nose, trying to pick up any scents.

There were none.

After a second, he headed back to the hide and went in, pushing aside the flap. He carefully put the hamper down near Liz.

'I think there may be some deer out there,' he said.

Liz gave a single grunt to acknowledge she'd heard

him, her full attention on the monitors.

Gary proffered a thermos…

Liz reached for it—

And in one quick move, the rear ceiling seam of the hide ripped open. Gary was grabbed by the collar, began a yell, and was hauled out of the hide.

Liz heard clothing and flesh being slashed apart by something razor-sharp. Gary's scream cut off abruptly. Then she heard low growls and feeding sounds outside.

Liz's brain caught up with what was happening. She stood, realised she was powerless and froze. She knew it was too late for Gary. And any second now, whatever it was that took him was going to come back for her.

She panicked. She had to get away, somewhere safe! The trees? Could she make it?

She raced to the hide window and, somehow, got herself through it. She landed on the ground, rolled to her feet and sprinted away from the hide.

She fled to the nearest tall tree. Her breathing and the noise of Gary being eaten were the only sounds in the night.

Liz whipped off her belt and slipped it around the tree trunk. Using it as a grip, she started to climb. She was doing well. She made it to the first branch, high off the ground. Awkwardly securing herself to the tree one-handed, she pulled out her mobile phone and dialled nine-nine-nine. She tucked the phone under her chin, listening as she looped the belt around the tree again and kept climbing.

It seemed like forever before the phone was answered, but it must have only been a second or two.

'Emergency services. Which service do you

require? Police, fire or ambulance?'

Jesus, it was a relief to hear the voice!

'All of them! Something just killed my husband.'

The next branch up was awkward. It blocked her way.

'What's your location, Ma'am?'

As Liz tried to find a way past the branch, she realised that the noises had stopped. She looked back at the hide. The phone slipped from under her chin and fell to the ground.

A dark shadow stood before the tent. Feline, nightmarish, huge, somehow the wrong shape.

Did it have wings?

Black against black. She couldn't make out details in the darkness, but its reflective eyes were locked on hers.

The Grim padded forward, watching her.

Liz gave a terrified squeak. She put all her effort into the climb. Legs locked around the trunk. She unlooped the belt, bit on it, hands free.

On the ground, the mobile chirped, 'Ma'am? Ma'am?'

Liz reached for a precarious handhold. Swung out. She somehow managed to get her free hand to another grip. She looked up; she should be able to get past the branch now. She looped her belt around the trunk again.

The Grim sped up its pace, leapt for her, spread its wings, flapped once …

Liz heard the sound and started to react—

Claws ripped into flesh and wood.

It was on her back, anchored to her and the tree. It sank its teeth into her throat before she could scream. The shock, as much as the injury, killed her. She went limp.

The Grim changed its grip, grasped her wrist in its powerful leathery hand and dropped her corpse to the ground. Then it let go of the tree, opened its wings and swooped down in a lazy circle, landing next to her corpse.

It lifted Liz by the shoulders, as a lover might, and sank its teeth back into her throat. It started to drink.

It was early morning in Princetown and few people were up. Baxter gleefully checked over his equipment on the Humvee. He was fairly bouncing with excited anticipation. Shane and Mabel cooled their heels by the Land Rover. Mabel fumed gently.

'He's a bit keen,' Shane observed.

'The footprints yesterday? This animal just upgraded itself from "same-old, same-old" cat hunt and brief news story to a "unique trophy and several talk show interviews" at the very least.'

Shane checked to see if she was joking. She wasn't.

Emma, a young local environmentalist, barely twenty, wearing a "ban hunting" sweatshirt, caught Mabel's attention and beckoned to her.

Mabel casually sauntered over.

In hushed tones, Emma said, 'You've always supported us, you love animals. How, in good conscience, you can help these people…?'

'I've got to. It's been made clear I have no choice.' Mabel's anger was obvious. They shared an outraged look.

Mabel stalked back to Shane. Phil arrived, with a strong coffee in one hand and a Danish pastry on a paper napkin in the other. Mabel's anger changed to sympathy.

'You look knackered.'

'I had an early start this morning; I've been up since three.' He unhappily dragged a tired hand through his hair. 'It got two of the cat fanatics. Night-vision cameras everywhere and not a trace of it. May as well be a ghost.' His phone rang. 'Hang on.'

Baxter strode over, toting his favourite rifle. Phil handed Baxter the coffee so that he could answer his phone. Baxter slurped the coffee but Phil didn't notice.

'Thanks!' Baxter saw the Danish in Phil's other hand and took the pastry.

Phil relinquished it as he concentrated on the call. Baxter scoffed the pastry and continued drinking the coffee.

Phil finished with the call. 'Okay. Thanks for letting me know.' He then realised his breakfast had been shanghaied. Baxter didn't notice Phil's distress.

Unbelievable! thought Shane, shaking his head. Then said, 'Well, at least we know where to start searching.'

'Dean Wood,' Phil confirmed.

'There's a thermos in the footwell,' Mabel offered. She indicated the Land Rover passenger seat.

Phil gratefully went after the drink.

They all got into the Land Rover. Luckily, Mabel had cleared the junk off the back seats the previous day, so there was enough room for them all. They drove off with Mabel at the wheel. Baxter and Shane were in good spirits, but Phil was pissed off about his breakfast. He wanted to be in bed. Shane checked the circled areas on the map, as Phil drank coffee.

In Dean Wood, a slender ribbon of silver birch and willow trees picked out the course of the river.

Shane kept an eye on it as he led the others along a trail through the woods, following the tracks of the beast. The last thing he wanted was to get them snared in a loop, surrounded by water on three sides and the beast corralling them in on the fourth. But he was becoming sure it wasn't interested in them at the moment, purely because he was fairly certain it wasn't even in the area any more.

Phil, clearly crotchety, stifled a yawn.

Shane stopped suddenly and cast about looking for the trail. He had lost the footprints; they just vanished. He shrugged to the others apologetically.

A few hours later, having found no new sign, they gave up and decided to return to the Land Rover. At last they could see it, parked a short distance ahead.

Baxter lengthened his stride and caught up to Mabel.

'You can't still be cross,' Baxter asked.

He put his hand on her shoulder. Mabel shrugged it off.

'Get your hands off me, you butcher!'

'What…?'

'You murder every animal you ever meet! For once in your life, can you stop being so bloody selfish and consider doing something for someone else? Hmm? Trap it! Don't kill it, trap it! Take it back to the zoo!'

'It's not that simple, lass.'

'Oh no, it never is with you! You want its head mounted on your wall. Another trophy. That's all you care about!'

'I care about you.'

'If you cared about me, that hunting park in Africa would be a nature reserve!' It was great to finally get the chance to vent her anger about the injustice and the betrayal she felt. 'I spent months of my life securing that land for us. Then you altered the planning paperwork and used the money I raised for the park to bribe an official so you could stick a hunting lodge in the middle of it! I can't believe what an arrogant, sneaky bastard you are. And—'

Phil interrupted her mid-rant. 'Will you shut up!'

She turned on him, her anger muting to dangerous reasonability.

'I don't want to be here. I don't want to be doing this. But *you* gave me no choice. And now you're saying I'm not allowed to talk?'

Phil restrained himself from trying to strangle her. 'I can't deal with you right now. I need sleep.'

He strode back to Land Rover, got in and slammed the door.

Baxter pointed to the Land Rover, indicating Mabel's rifle locked in its mounting.

'So, I'm flawed. You're no saint! You don't use a baby like that for fooling about with rabbits. That'd take your head clean off.'

'The rifle?' *Why did she have to explain this; he was impossible!* 'If a deer has a broken leg, I'm expected to take care of it. It's kinder than letting nature take its course and it's part of my job.'

'Any excuse to fire a loaded weapon. Don't start giving me this wounded conservationist bullshit. You loved the rifle range.'

'Paper targets are very different and you know it!'

Baxter thought about the difference and then remembered his latest kill. 'Mmm.'

Mabel knew what he was imagining. Furious, she stomped away and got in to the Land Rover with Phil, trying not to disturb him.

Baxter's gaze followed her. He was confused. He couldn't see the difference. One target was as good as another, but a moving target was more of a challenge – and he loved to win.

The morning was over; lunch had been eaten. Mabel, Phil, Baxter and Shane had driven around, checking different locations for any sign of the beast. Shane ticked those places off on his list.

Now the Land Rover was parked up in a roadside bay. Phil was asleep in the passenger seat; the others had decided they should let him rest. A note had been taped to the window in case he should wake: "Gone to Belstone Nine Stones. Back soon."

Mabel looked down from her vantage point on the tor. She could just make out Phil as he slept in the front. She looked at the others; they were making good progress. She stretched her limbs, then set out again, climbing after them.

At the top of Belstone Nine Stones, Shane continued to scout for evidence. Mabel and Baxter looked around trying to spot any clues as to whether the beast had been there, but saw nothing.

Their next stop was a National Trust parking lot by the small village of Lydford. A signpost proudly pointed to White Lady Waterfall via two routes, either the "long and easy" path, or the "short and steep" path. Below were additional signs for The Gorge and the Devil's Cauldron.

In the Land Rover, Phil shifted position and went

back to sleep. This note taped to the window read: "Back soon." They didn't need to state where they were, he couldn't fail to miss the signposts.

Lydford Gorge, with its Devil's Cauldron and White Lady Waterfall, were a classic natural attraction for the tourists, but this late in the season there were only a few hardy souls to be seen – painting students and their teacher, all hard at work at their easels.

Shane, Mabel and Baxter looked around. Again they found no trace of the beast. They didn't really expect to here; too many people for a wild animal to be comfortable. Then again, if it wasn't scared of people… That's why they checked.

Despite finding nothing, the pleasant walk was reward enough for Mabel. It was beautiful there and she took full advantage of the lack of crowds to lag behind a bit and enjoy drinking in the scenery of Lydford Gorge by herself.

The Land Rover was parked up in another roadside parking spot. The high moorland scenery gave good vantage over the barren, grass-covered, rock-infested slopes that stretched towards the horizon. Phil, in a different position, snored gently. The note taped to the window read: "Gone to Great Mis Tor. Back soon."

On Great Mis Tor, Shane, Mabel and Baxter looked around.

The Land Rover stood in a parking bay in Foxworthy. Phil snored, shifted position, then stopped snoring. The note taped to the window read: "Gone to Harton Chest and Hunter's Tor. Back soon."

The steep walk up to Hunters Tor had revealed some wonderful scenery, but no sign of the beast. By the time the group reached Harton Chest it was mid-afternoon and they had done enough exercise to last them a week, but there was more to do yet. They had a quick look around, but again Shane and Baxter found no trace of anything larger than a badger.

In the Land Rover, Phil was in a different position. He slept quietly. The note taped to the window read: "Gone to Wistman's Wood. Back soon."

At Wistman's Wood, Shane, Mabel and Baxter looked around.

The Land Rover was parked in another gravel-paved tourist parking zone, but now it was empty.

On the Pipe Walk and Dewerstone woodland path, Shane, Mabel, Phil and Baxter looked around, but again found no trace.

Everyone looked around the Avon Dam Reservoir and came away empty-handed.

It was sunset and they were back near Princetown, on Foggin Tor. The granite cliff of the disused quarry curved away above them. The hunters stood below the bluff. Shane, relaxed but alert, scanned the scenery; Mabel, cross but keeping her temper in check, glared at the rocky ground; Phil covered a yawn; Baxter, keen, alert, high on adrenaline, went to investigate some scuff marks in the dusty gravel trail.

Phil looked at Baxter. 'Doesn't he ever get tired?' he asked Mabel.

'No,' she replied.

Above them, a small rock dislodged and bounced down; its impacts scattered more small rocks on the scree slope. The noise made them all jump. Four pairs of eyes scanned the area.

Silent, they signalled one another, co-ordinating their search. They checked around, looking from different angles. There was nothing visible there that might have caused the rock to slip. Despite their scrutiny, they all came up empty.

They regrouped and looked out over the darkening landscape. A ground mist curled in the low-lying areas. Aside from that, there was nothing to see but a few sheep snoozing in the twilight. After a while Baxter pulled out the map. Phil stifled another yawn. The map had a number of places on it that had been carefully circled and then crossed out by Shane.

'Where next?' Baxter enquired.

Each of the others gave him a look. Mabel ground her teeth.

'It's fucking dark. Let's start again tomorrow.'

'She's right,' said Shane. 'We can't search properly in this. There are too many crags and crevices that we'll miss.'

Baxter looked speculatively at the immediate landscape. 'I'm going to camp here. Get a proper feel for the territory,' he stated.

Shane thought he was nuts.

'Your choice,' said Mabel. She turned to Phil and Shane. 'Come on.'

'Six a.m. tomorrow?' suggested Baxter.

'Eight,' Shane responded.

Phil smiled and shook his head, 'Seven.'

Shane, Baxter and Mabel settled for Phil's compromise. Once the start time had been agreed, they all walked back down the track.

Mabel had been trying to think of a way to save the

big cat all day, but she remembered Ms Smith's corpse, and now it had killed the two videographers as well. There had to be a way to make it harmless; a way to save this undiscovered species. As they were nearing the vehicles she finally asked Phil, 'Do we really have to kill this thing?'

'Mabel, we can't let it keep killing people.'

She raised her voice, trying to persuade all of them. 'So trap it? Once it's in a cage it won't be a danger anymore.'

They got to the Humvee and Baxter started to pull out his camping gear. 'Lass, a keeper wouldn't be able to go anywhere near it. You know how it works. If they develop the taste, they don't go back. Three people? This one has developed a taste.'

'But it's an innocent animal,' Mabel pleaded.

She could see pleading wasn't working so she changed tack. She knew Baxter's weaknesses so she played to them instead.

'It's unusual. Unique. Far more valuable alive than dead.' She could see he was listening. 'Everyone would want to come and see it. Scientists, the general public, the media.' She'd nearly hooked him. 'Someone would need to give it a home, talk to people about it, give interviews, tell the world.' Mabel could tell Baxter was thinking about it.

The idea caught him for a moment, but this would be a big commitment and he didn't want to be tied down.

'I've been hired to shoot it.' He'd made his decision. 'I'm going to shoot it.'

Baxter picked up his gear and set off back up the path, leaving Shane, Mabel and Phil to walk to the Land Rover in the twilight.

Phil got into the passenger seat and made himself comfortable.

Shane took a last look over the landscape, while Mabel stowed their gear.

Shane sensed something. He didn't know what, but suddenly his senses were sharpened, alert. What caused that? Was it a scent on the breeze? Shane didn't know, but he followed his instincts. He was in full hunter mode, homing in on the target, tracking the smallest signs of movement in the distance.

Finally his search was rewarded, he spotted it. The creature was partially screened from his sight by bushes, but he glimpsed it as it loped over a ridge and out of sight again. Not taking his eyes from the spot, Shane grabbed Mabel's shirt.

He said in a low whisper, 'It's here.'

She reacted, bolt upright, and tried to pinpoint what had caught his attention.

He pointed and spoke softly, 'Up wind, hasn't smelt us. Keep quiet.'

Mabel eased open the passenger door and whispered, 'Phil!'

He was dozing off and didn't hear her so she tried again a little louder.

'Phil!'

'What?' he mumbled, reacting groggily.

She hushed him, then said in a low voice, 'It just went over that ridge.'

'Get your rifle,' murmured Shane.

'No,' she replied. 'I don't want to see this. I'm going home.'

Phil, wide awake now, didn't like the idea for lots of reasons. He stated the most obvious one first, 'You can't, you're our driver.'

Mabel threw Shane the keys.

'Fine. I'll walk home.'

Shane stared at her in disbelief.

'Hold up! It's too far. And what if that bloody thing comes after you? You'll be safer with us.'

Mabel couldn't argue with that and she was not happy about it.

They followed an animal track through the low trees, bushes and knee-length heather. Shane led the way; Phil and Mabel snuck along as quietly as they could behind him. Shane crouched and motioned them down. They crouched too. Mabel closed her mobile phone.

'I can't raise Baxter,' she said quietly. 'He's switched off his phone.'

In the distance a dark shape prowled through the scrub.

Shane waved them forward as he rose and continued to stalk the beast.

The creature paused and turned its head.

Shane signalled *halt* and froze. The others complied.

It hadn't seen them. It scented the air, paused, and then reacted to something they couldn't see. It loped forward quickly over the next rise and was lost from sight.

They continued to sneak forward as quietly and quickly as they could. At last they reached the rise and peered over.

The scrub turned into woodland in the sheltered river valley that lay beyond. There was no sign of the animal.

'Where did it go?' asked Phil.

Shane pointed. There were traces of disturbed ground where it had passed: bent grass and a faint imprint in the soil. The trees ahead cast deep shadows in the half-light of near dark. They followed the trail into this blackness.

They stalked silently, Shane still leading the way. He unclipped his hunter's torch-lamp from his belt, twisted it to a shuttered, narrow beam, aimed it at the ground and switched it on. It illuminated only the smallest part of the trail, allowing him to follow the faintest telltale signs.

Crack. The noise was small, but it was a total giveaway. Had it heard? They reacted with a mixture of fear and trepidation. Phil looked down at the twig he'd just stepped on. They waited in total silence for heart-pounding seconds, listening.

Nothing.

After a long moment, Shane led them off again. But as they moved, Shane heard the faintest noise. A footfall? And again, accompanied by the swish of branches as something shadowed them as they walked.

In one swift movement, Shane cocked his gun, turned and aimed with both torch and rifle.

Phil and Mabel reacted, turning as they tried to bring up their weapons. Phil got a bead – and relaxed.

The light revealed Baxter, arm up to protect his eyes. Mabel stifled a swearword.

'Hi,' he whispered quietly.

Baxter joined Shane.

'Where is it?' he asked.

'Up that way, half a mile, I think,' Shane replied.

Baxter nodded.

A woman's scream pierced the night.

Shane switched his torch to wide beam, illuminating the night as he, Baxter and Phil sprinted towards the noise. A moment later, Mabel chased after them.

A grassy field flanked a shallow rock-strewn river gully. There were eight tents pitched in various places across the field. At the campsite, three fires had burned down to glowing embers. The inhabitants of the tents were either asleep or had been indulging in romance.

Beside the river, seventeen-year-old Beauty, spattered with her fiancé's blood, whimpered. A powerful, black-furred hand with elongated fingers pinned her to the ground.

Next to her, The Grim dropped the young man's corpse, then leaned in close, intimate, and looked at her for a long moment. It gave a slow grin; enjoying her terror. The Grim brought up its hand – slowly long claws snicked into place one by one.

Beauty couldn't tear her eyes away.

The Grim ran its fingers gently down her torso, rested its hand on her stomach. Then, snake-like, it angled its head and looked enquiringly into her eyes. Beauty realised its intent, and a tear slid down her cheek.

The Grim tensed.

Beauty's whimper became a scream as her expression contorted with pain. The scream choked off in a gurgle of blood.

Her body jerked as The Grim ripped its hand up through her ribcage. It licked her blood off its arm. Then it turned its head to look appraisingly at the tents. Swift as a shadow, it darted forward.

Bill, partially clothed, clutching a wooden mallet, stumbled past the last tent towards the river, peering through the dark. The Grim landed on his chest: a patch of solid, lethal darkness knocking him to the ground. It sprang away again for the nearest tent. James and Conrad pulled the collapsible support pole free of the entrance. They rapidly split it back into its component parts to be used as weapons. Bill lay where he fell, his chest and neck slashed to ribbons. He clutched at his throat, futilely trying to stop the blood flow. The sounds and noises of the others echoed across the moor as they rose and responded to the horror unfolding around them.

Maddy exited her tent, bewildered and scared. She could only watch as The Grim slaughtered James. Conrad screamed and tried to stab the beast with the tent pole. The Grim slashed a gaping fatal wound into Conrad with one blow. He fell lifeless to the grass. Maddy couldn't draw a breath, couldn't move. Terror rooted her to the spot.

The Grim saw the effect of her terror and gave a deep, throaty, inhuman chuckle as it stalked towards her. Closer. Closer. Halfway to her. Then it abruptly darted sideways towards a nearby tent. Its claws sheared through the canvas.

A yell and a scream from inside.

The Grim pulled Hanna headfirst from the dwelling and bit down on her throat. As it drank, it plunged its arm back into the tent. Gordon, who was scrambling out of the exit, was dragged back in and then pulled through the rip; he dangled face to face with The Grim. It held Gordon fast as he screamed and struggled, fighting against the monster, clawing and hitting at its arm. The Grim finished with Hanna, dropped her body and pinned Gordon's arms against his sides in a merciless embrace, then pulled him in for another vampire-kiss.

People running from the tents, saw the carnage and reacted with varying degrees of horror and panic. The Grim moved among them. Their torches were knocked to the ground; one still had a severed hand attached. Fleeting, invisible as a wraith, black death struck over and over, putting out any light, keeping the night dark.

Baxter hurdled a fallen tree trunk. Phil, Shane and Mabel were in hot pursuit.

They heard more screams fill the night. Shouts. Hysteria. Panic stifled as death struck again and again.

Maddy, knuckles white, gripped the tent pole. She was shaking with fear. Around her in the night she heard the sounds of people dying and glimpsed The Grim as it attacked its victims, people she knew well.

It used its claws to hamstring Richard as he tried to flee. He screamed in pain and fell, feet useless. The beast left him, turned away and killed another. Richard wanted to run, but all he could do was crawl.

It killed again and again. Until, at last, silence descended.

The only noises were of Maddy's ragged breathing and Richard pulling himself towards the trees.

The Grim padded towards Maddy, eyes fixed on its prey.

She couldn't make her body move. Tears of frustration and terror filled her eyes.

It watched her as she stood rooted to the spot, gripping the tent pole, shaking with terror. And it smiled.

'Run. Need to run,' she told herself. She let go of the pole and clutched at her leg, pulling to lift it. 'Move, damn it!' she sobbed. 'Move!' She lifted her leg, put it down. A step! She pulled at the other, lifted it, put it down. 'Yes! Run! Need to run!'

Finally her brain took control. Stiff-legged she tottered away. She was gaining ground. Then she felt the claws on her shoulder!

The Grim turned her around to face it. The beast looked down at her and smiled. Then its tongue slowly licked a fang.

'No?' Maddy didn't mean it to be a question, then realised she was asking God or Fate or some higher power for help. Help she knew wouldn't come.

Richard grabbed a young hawthorn trunk and pulled himself over the low earth and rock boundary into the bracken and trees.

Behind him, The Grim on all fours, finished its meal, looked up, then stepped over Maddy's corpse and loped slowly after Richard.

Richard, hands scratched and bloody, grunted with effort as he pulled himself around rocks and trees, past bushes and deeper into the woodland. He reached for his next handhold. But The Grim landed on his back, driving the breath out of his body.

Shane and the others ran full pelt through the trees. The last scream gurgled out. This ominous silence was somehow worse.

They broke cover as the trees abruptly gave way to a grassy field and a shallow, rock-strewn river gully.

The sight that greeted them was of ripped up tents and the carnage of mutilated human bodies.

Shane, Baxter, Mabel and Phil came to a halt as they took it all in. Mabel stumbled over to Bill to see if she could help. She checked for vital signs, but he had already bled to death. Baxter clamped a hand over his mouth. This was too much horror to fully comprehend in one instant.

Phil checked for survivors. His emotions had shut down and his mind had switched to autopilot in order to allow him to function. Shane scanned the area then checked the tree line for any sign of It. Mabel, kneeling by Bill, looked around at the chaos. She met Phil's shocked gaze.

'Dead,' she confirmed, swallowing back the bile that threatened to rise in her throat. 'You'll need to send in the mop up crew.'

'Yeah,' Phil responded. '…Yeah.' He pulled out his phone.

Shane spoke to Baxter, 'Can you see it? Where did it go?'

'It can't have got far,' he replied.

They took a moment to deal with the shock. Then, weapons held at the ready, Shane, Baxter and Mabel checked the area. Meanwhile Phil called forensics.

Baxter followed the beast's tracks toward the river gully. Mabel noticed the trail of blood that led into the woods. She cautiously followed it.

Shane muttered to himself, 'A lion did this?'

Mabel shouted, 'Over here!' to get their attention.

Shane followed her when he saw what she was up to. He covered the distance quickly, but she crossed the boundary into the woods before he had quite reached her side.

Mabel clutched her rifle. She checked back to make sure Shane was following. He was.

There was an obvious trail of blood and broken plants ahead. Despite her fear, she forged on to see if she was in time to be able to help the person.

Shane's jacket got snagged by the hawthorn. He quietly set about untangling himself, raised his torch now and then to keep an eye on Mabel and the woods.

Peering all around, wary of attack, Mabel investigated the undergrowth around her as she followed the blood trail.

A clump of bushes blocked her way; the trail led around them. On the far side her torch revealed Richard. He was definitely dead.

Mabel stooped for a closer look. Her senses jangled. She looked up—

—The Grim was in mid pounce!

It made sure its landing drove the torch from her hand. Mabel's yell cut off before it started as the impact of The Grim's body knocked the air out of her. Its weight bore her to the ground.

She stared up into a mouth full of fangs. She was pinned. Defenceless.

The Grim crouched over her. It smiled. Then used a single claw to slice open her cheek. It leaned in close and slowly lapped her blood. Mabel whimpered. The Grim snarled. She froze.

At the noise, Shane looked up. There was no sign of Mabel. His torch only revealed bushes and trees. He ran forward. Unnoticed, his jacket ripped as his momentum pulled it free of the ensnaring thorns. He fired into the air as he went.

Baxter and Phil looked towards the shot. They pounded towards the boundary. Nearly there.

The Grim licked more blood from Mabel's cheek. It looked her in the eyes, then at her throat, then back to her eyes.

Mabel was already terrified; she didn't need it playing with her – *its food*, her brain helpfully filled in – like this. She suddenly felt very sorry for mice.

A gentle, rumbling purr. It enjoyed knowing that she knew.

Bastard, she thought.

It shifted back a little, lowered its snout. Its velvet nose-fur tickled her skin as it moved its mouth down towards her jugular.

Shane cleared the bushes. The torchlight hit The Grim revealing it for a split second. It hissed, reared up and sprang away. He shot it.

Hurtling through the woods, Phil fired into the air. Baxter levelled his rifle and shot at it too, but it was already gone, vanished into the night.

Mabel lay on the ground. As shock kicked in she started to shake.

Shane helped Mabel up. She was shaky as hell. He held her, wrapping her in his jacket.

Phil and Baxter scanned the area. Baxter tried to find its eyes in the dark. But it was gone.

'I can't have missed,' Baxter asserted.

'That was *not* a cat,' Mabel said.

Shane got the first aid kit out and tended to her wound. Meanwhile, Baxter checked around for a blood trail or any indication it was hit.

'What was it?' Phil asked them.

Mabel looked angry.

'Whatever it was, we need to kill it.'

Phil knew he shouldn't have been surprised by her

reaction, but the conservationist he'd always loved seemed to have fled when it came to this creature. He would have to report the additional attack. He got out his phone.

'What did it look like?' Baxter asked, unable to hide his excitement.

'Big, black, teeth like that,' Her fingers said *The teeth were this big!* 'and... wings.' She couldn't believe she was saying it. 'It had fucking wings!'

Baxter looked at her suspiciously.

'You gone mad?' he asked, a note of concern in his voice.

Mabel wasn't listening to him, instead asking herself aloud, 'Some kind of demon, maybe?'

'It's the fear, lass. You were hallucinating. The mind can play terrible tricks. It's just a bloody big black leopard gone kill-crazy.'

'That's not what I saw!' She was adamant.

Phil paced a bit further until he finally got a connection on his mobile. It was answered almost immediately. 'Larry? Send a sniper unit as well. The team will need some protection from this thing.'

Baxter shook his head. 'I can't believe we all missed it!'

In the darkness of the early hours of the morning the Humvee and Land Rover drove quietly into town and parked.

In one of the anti-hunt bannered campervans Lorraine looked up from her route planning and checked who had arrived.

Protective, Shane helped Mabel from the Land Rover,

taking care to be quiet. Baxter exited the Humvee without any thought for the sleeping locals and joined them.

Baxter patted Mabel on the shoulder. 'You did good, girl.'

Mabel controlled her desire to snarl and hit him. Her brief, placatory smile was more of a grimace.

Shane distracted her by saying, 'We'll continue this tomorrow.' To Baxter, 'I'll take her home.'

Baxter agreed. 'Seven a.m. Here.'

Shane acknowledged him and Baxter walked away, heading for the comfort of his rented rooms.

Once he was gone, Shane looked at Mabel and said seriously, 'What you saw – we need to talk about it.' She nodded. 'My place?' he asked.

'You still got that whisky?'

Shane smiled. 'Yeah. Good idea.'

They headed towards his house, but Lorraine intercepted them. She was civilised but intent on convincing Mabel to abandon the hunt for the beast.

'Emma told me you were helping these arseholes.'

Mabel rounded on her. 'You don't let a rabid beast live!' she said vehemently.

Lorraine couldn't believe she'd just heard Mabel say that; she was left gob-smacked as Mabel strode away.

Shane caught up with Mabel as they continued to walk towards his place. 'Are you alright?' he enquired.

'This thing is going down. And it *is* a thing. It's evil. I looked in its eyes. It was tormenting me. It knows what it's doing. It was having fun. Fuck saving the fluffy bunnies, this thing has to die! Whatever it takes.'

'What I saw back there, I only glimpsed 'un, but you're right. That was no black leopard.'

Shane opened the door for her. They entered his house.

It was a welcoming home, cosy, clean, well-loved by Shane and previous generations.

'Definitely not a big cat,' agreed Mabel. She followed him into the kitchen.

Shane nodded thoughtfully. 'I'll get us a drink and then I'll tell you a story. Make yourself at home.'

Mabel sat at the ancient, homemade kitchen table. Shane plonked the beverages down and joined her.

'Are you sitting comfortably? Then I shall begin.'

Mabel looked askance at him.

Shane continued, unabashed, 'When I was little, my Granny used to tell me stories about The Grim.' He took a sip of whisky. ''Un was a creature made from the night itself, wings like a bat, teeth like a cat, claws long as your finger.'

Mabel pulled her glass towards her.

'She said 'un slept in a cave under the cliff on Crag Tor. But every hundred years or so 'un woke up, fierce hungry. And it would come down from the moor, killing dogs and horses and men.' He looked up, meeting her eyes. 'If The Grim wakes up, don't go out after dark, she'd say.' Shane took another sip of his whisky. ''Un could change shape, slip through the smallest crack, run fast as the wind and silent as the grave. Old Bradley, he said 'un was a Wish Hound from the Devil's pack. Granny said, no, 'un was worse.'

'Did she say how to kill it?'

'Never did mention that.' He turned his glass. 'When the killing stopped, she said the local Bishop claimed credit, but she reckoned 'un had just had its fill of blood and gone back to sleep in its cave under the cliff.'

'Crag Tor?' Mabel considered, then said, 'That place is riddled with mine shafts.'

'Yep.'

'It's a place to start.'

They mulled this over.

After a moment Mabel spoke, 'Your spare Winchester two-seventy, can I borrow it?'

'Yep.'

The following morning, Shane dressed in his usual poaching greens, but this time on top of that he also wore some military grade, army surplus body armour and a double thickness Kevlar jacket with a high collar, currently open and folded down so he could move his neck freely. In addition, slung across his torso were two powerful rifles, one with telescopic sights, along with a spare ammunition belt and a rope.

A sheathed hunting knife sat at his hip and long chain mail fishing gloves were hooked through the other side of his belt. A small backpack, plus a fully-stocked climber's belt and gear weighed him down even further, but, since he knew the area they were going to, he'd deemed them essential. On his head a potholing helmet finished the ensemble. Shane meant business.

He entered Princetown Church, which was thankfully deserted. Shane approached the font and simultaneously dipped a colourful high-powered water gun and a large water bottle into it. When they were full he stoppered them carefully, then strode out.

The town square was a hive of activity as people moved to and fro. In the background, the army were setting up a base and sending out "search and destroy" teams onto the moor.

Baxter scowled at the military operation in progress as he crossed to greet Phil, then eyed up the five police marksmen who were with him. Phil introduced them: Bill, Jim, Harry, Dave and Tom. Each had a large kitbag full of gear. Baxter wasn't happy about this additional help.

He gestured towards the army. 'It's bad enough we have to put up with them fouling the tracks.' He indicated the marksmen. 'We don't need these guys too.'

'After our great success yesterday?' Phil asked sarcastically. 'I thought we could use the extra firepower. The more eyes, the more chance of killing the beast.'

Mabel arrived.

Baxter shook his head and voiced his thoughts, 'More chance of giving away our position and scaring it off, you mean.'

By the look Phil gave him, Baxter knew he had no choice.

'Alright,' Baxter capitulated. 'But the corpse is mine!'

'Yes, yes.' Phil smiled, one battle over, 'Whatever you want.'

Mabel eyed the marksmen sceptically.

Tom saw her look. 'Don't worry, Miss. We'll take care of it,' he said confidently.

Mabel remained unconvinced.

'It will have moved after yesterday,' Baxter chimed in. 'Any ideas where to start today?'

'Crag Tor,' supplied Mabel. 'Lots of caves and old mine shafts. If it's hiding, good chance it'll be there.'

Baxter checked the map and thought about it. 'Yes,' he agreed. He looked at Mabel with renewed appreciation. 'You're a brave lass with a good brain. Why you aren't married yet I don't know.'

'Because I have a brain, Baxter.'

The marksmen pretended they weren't listening.

'Oh come on lass, we were good together.'

'No, you patronising, devious, self-serving bastard! We weren't.'

Baxter, upset, looked for a source of distraction, then spotted Shane heading over. He chuckled. 'What do you look like?'

The marksmen saw Shane's gear and hid their amusement.

Tom smothered a grin and said, 'Nice helmet.'

Shane assessed them coolly, noting the body language and stance each of them used, along with any calluses that could betray obvious skills which they may possess. They looked as though they could handle themselves, but he'd reserve judgement until he knew them better.

Baxter noticed the water pistol and laughed out loud.

'Holy water,' said Shane. 'Just in case.'

'In case of what?' asked Phil incredulously.

'In case 'un's not a big cat.'

Baxter rolled his eyes. 'What the hell else would it be?'

Mabel gave him a level look and said, 'You don't want to know.'

Shane answered him, 'Pure evil?'

'Yeah, right,' snorted Baxter. 'And what's this?' He pulled on a string around Shane's neck, revealing a garlic necklace.

'Boy Scouts' motto: "be prepared".'

Baxter started laughing. 'Jeeze! This isn't a vampire hunt!' He controlled himself, damping down the laughter into a faint smile, then feigned sober interest as he dug deeper. 'What else ya got?'

Shane was happy to reply. They needed to appreciate what they were up against. 'Salt. A potent remedy against evil.'

The marksmen covered up their reactions. Phil wasn't sure how to react.

'What?' Shane asked, the wide-eyed innocent.

'Nothing,' said Phil.

Baxter gave his opinion, 'You are one superstitious dude.'

A smile crinkled the corner of Shane's lips, betraying his deadpan reply, 'I'm a seasoned hunter.'

The marksmen weren't sure what to make of this man. Phil grinned.

Shane handed Mabel one of his rifles.

Bill asked, 'You know how to use that?'

Mabel gave him a withering look.

Introductions done, Baxter's excitement made him impatient to get going. 'Let's go get this cat!'

Phil and Tom went with Baxter in his Humvee. Bill, Jim, Harry and Dave got into their police issue off-roader. Shane went with Mabel. The convoy drove out of town, Mabel's Land Rover leading the way.

It was late morning by the time they reached the

logger's track. The convoy sped up the wooded hillside along the dirt and gravel road until they reached a turning circle. They parked up along its edge, on the boundary where open space met the crowding trees.

Mabel and the other experienced hunters couldn't help but remember the horrors of the night before. They could virtually feel the unforgiving, deep shadow under the forestry pine as it waited silently for them. Its darkness started just a few feet in under the canopy.

A footpath led steeply upwards, through what would eventually turn out to be a narrow band of increasingly stunted trees. This strip of woodland separated the turning circle from the main bulk of Crag Tor. The top of it lay high enough to sit above the natural tree line. As they all got out of the vehicles, each of them grabbed their gear, ready for the long walk to the cave system.

Baxter surreptitiously sneaked a brick-sized parcel from under his passenger seat, and muttered to himself, 'Try chewing on this,' as he put it into his pack.

They all headed off up the forest footpath, in single file, with varying degrees of excitement, boredom or cautious trepidation. Long before noon, Mabel and Shane had led the group up out of the wind-stunted trees to where the footpath met the barren slopes of Crag Tor. Boulders and scree fought the short grass and stunted blueberry bushes for dominance of the area, below a forbidding natural cliff that stretched away.

Shane and Baxter cast around for any trace of the beast's footprints. It didn't take long for Shane to find a trail. They set off. Baxter, excited but cautious; Shane, Mabel and Phil with varying degrees of nervousness; the marksmen cocky and a little bored.

It didn't take long to get to The Grim's hidey-hole. Two cave entrances snuggled near each other under the cliff.

'Which one?' asked Tom.

Baxter spotted a print. 'This one.'

'Are you certain?' Phil asked.

Baxter pointed at another print behind a stunted blueberry bush that Phil hadn't detected. The marksmen perked up. Mabel breathed deeply to calm herself. They stationed themselves near the entrance.

'I have a little present for each of you,' said Shane, as he pulled a bag of glow sticks from his rucksack.

In answer, the marksmen got out their night-vision goggles.

Tom held some out. 'We brought some spares,' he offered.

He chucked the night-vision goggles to Mabel, Phil, Baxter and Shane in turn. Shane hung his off his belt. ''Un doesn't attack in daylight,' he stated. 'Maybe there's a reason?'

Baxter stared at him. 'You're embarrassing to know.'

Shane handed several glow sticks to each member of the team anyway. 'We're going underground. Something goes wrong with these,' Shane tapped the goggles, 'and you don't have any extra light? Could be unpleasant.'

Baxter didn't want to hear it.

Shane saw this and asked, 'You ever done any potholing?'

Baxter hadn't.

'Caving?' Shane asked.

Baxter hadn't done that either.

'Then take the light and pay attention.'

'Give me the bag!' Baxter was annoyed.

Shane passed him the bag of glow sticks. 'Don't lose it.'

Tom cleared his throat. 'This is an old mine, right?'

'Yes, there is a cave system here as well.'

Tom smiled at Shane. 'So, we're looking at a labyrinth, cold, dark, possible drops, likely flooding?'

'Um, yes. That just about covers 'un.'

'Fine. We're good to go then,' finished Tom. He shouldered his kitbag and, following his lead, the other marksmen did the same.

Baxter stopped them short. 'This…'

The marksmen paused.

'…man-eater, whatever species it is, is very, very fast.' Happy they were listening, he continued, 'It can see in the dark better than we can see in daylight, move silently and it is not afraid of us. That makes it extremely dangerous.'

As Baxter talked, Shane handed out salt pouches. The others looked at the pouches and investigated the contents.

'You're joking,' Bill murmured and tossed the bag of salt away.

Shane retrieved it and handed it back. 'We don't know what we're dealing with here. Better safe than sorry, ay?'

Bill shook his head.

Shane turned to Mabel, then he gently slapped her gun barrel. 'Steel? Should work the same against evil as cold iron.'

Mabel smiled weakly and swallowed.

They double-checked their gear and slowly walked underground.

The cave was just the entrance to what turned out to be a wide, man-made tunnel. They walked two abreast. Shane and Mabel took positions at the rear.

As they passed into the underground gloom, Bill dropped his bag of salt. Harry followed suit. But Dave clutched his gun tighter, looking at the walls and ceiling with anxiety. He couldn't hide his nervousness.

As the daylight receded, the marksmen put on their night-vision goggles. Infrared beams from each set of goggles criss-crossed the tunnel as the marksmen looked around.

The long entrance tunnel turned a corner into a small room. There were two other exits, both of which led into the mine. Ancient broken junk was scattered here and there around the floor and along the base of the walls. Anything useful was long gone. Twin sets of air and power ducts showed where a generator and a pump had once stood. The tubing vanished into the depths of each tunnel.

Mabel flicked on her torch. Bill swore as the marksmen all flinched and pulled their night-vision goggles away from their eyes.

'Turn that off!' ordered Tom. 'Use the N.V.D.s.'

'I'm not going in there without a light on.'

Baxter shook his head. 'What are you, three?' he mocked.

'You could stay outside?' Phil suggested.

'On my own? No way!'

'I'm not going in without a light on either,' said Shane. 'You'll have to live with it.'

Tom looked at him, then to Phil for a verdict. Phil

decided to let it ride for now. He shook his head.

Tom unwillingly agreed, 'Alright.' Then he turned to Harry and pointed at a spot on the wall by the entrance. 'Tag it.'

Harry got out some chalk and drew a big arrow, pointing back the way they had come, making sure he did the same at regular intervals along each of the tunnels and at every intersection and turn they travelled.

The marksmen sorted out their gear and pulled out the things that they thought they were likely to need, including their torches.

Shane unpacked a storm lantern and set it up.

Phil consulted his maps and, via torchlight, found the right one for this mine.

When Shane lit the storm lantern, the room flooded with friendly yellow light. He adjusted the lantern's shutters to reduce the glare a little and to focus the light forward in a 120 degree arc. Then he turned to Phil, 'Can I see that?'

Phil handed the map over.

'We could always net the thing?' Shane suggested. 'Block the tunnels so 'un can't escape. Kill it while it's all tangled up. This here says there's only the two entrances to the mine.'

'You think a bit of rope will stop an angry lion?' scoffed Baxter.

'Delay the beast a bit. Slow 'un down.'

'Waste of time,' said Baxter.

'We don't have a net,' Phil pointed out. 'Come on, we need to get moving.'

Shane scoured the map deeply. Once done, he handed it back.

Mabel sniffed the air. She thought she could smell

rotting flesh. 'Can anyone smell that?'

'Yep,' Shane confirmed.

Phil located their position on the map.

'Where are we?' Baxter asked. He took hold of a corner of the map and they looked at it together.

'Here, I think,' Phil pointed. Then, done looking, released the map to Baxter's curiosity.

Shane, following his nose, led them out of the room. 'Come on,' he called to them.

Baxter pocketed the map.

They followed Shane up a long, twisting passage. The storm lantern revealed a good stretch of the corridor ahead until it turned out of view.

Behind Shane, the others' torches picked out the person and the space in front of them. They were moving pools of light in the engulfing darkness.

Baxter looked at his watch, wondering how long it would take to reach the beast. 'How far in do you think it is?'

'Further than this,' Shane said unhelpfully.

In the distance up ahead, the illumination from the lantern revealed a sheep's leg at the side of the tunnel.

As they closed the gap, they could see there was a side tunnel. It was formed by natural, unhewn rock that ballooned out into an uneven cave, then narrowed and terminated in a wall of rubble. The rest of the sheep's carcass lay at the back of the cave, about a third of the way up the rubble slope. Beetles crawled over it, feeding.

Mabel could hear something. *Rustling?* 'Quiet!'

They heard a slight change in the acoustics of the cave, accompanied by a sense of movement; black against black. As they perceived both, they wondered, was it here? An adrenaline surge kicked in for each of them.

Shane swung the lantern up and around. A nest of bats – disturbed, unhappy – took off from the roof.

'Everyone stay still!' he shouted urgently, as the bats flew through the cavern and swooped out past them.

Dave screamed and dived to the floor, covering his head.

It was over in a moment. The others recovered from the shock.

'I hate bats!' said Dave loudly. 'Have they gone?'

'Yes,' Mabel said. She sounded much calmer than she felt.

Dave uncovered his head and shakily got to his feet. 'Sorry,' he said sheepishly.

Shane went to take a closer look at the rotting carcass. More beetles scavenged on something higher up the slope. He gingerly started climbing the rubble to get to it. It turned out to be another piece of sheep.

Tom, suspicion aroused, said, 'There's something odd about the echo in here.'

Shane shone his torch up to the top of the rubble wall and saw only blackness where it should meet the ceiling. He knew it meant that there was a gap, probably large enough to crawl through. He checked the space, then beckoned the others. 'It went this way.'

He started crawling through the low gap. The others lost sight of him. They quickly followed him up the slope, crawling after him through the shallow open channel between ceiling and floor.

Shane waited until the others had caught up with him. Phil helped Mabel clamber down a large boulder.

'I wonder how long it's been since anyone was down here?' Mabel asked, curious.

Baxter moved to one side to let Harry jump down and glass crunched under his boot. It was the remains of an ancient oil lamp. He picked up the corroded casing and dusted it off. There was a date: 1804.

'A long time,' he answered.

He chucked the casing to Phil, who took a look.

Baxter pulled out the map and, as he suspected, the cave system wasn't shown. 'This lot,' he gestured at the tunnel, 'isn't on here. I'll mark it as we go.' He pulled out a pencil and carefully started adding it in.

Phil leaned in to check the craftsmanship and was surprised to see Baxter's technical, very accurate mapping skills.

'You're good,' Phil complimented.

'I know.'

Mabel shook her head.

'Come on then,' said Shane, and set off again. The others followed him down the tunnel as he lit the way with the lantern. Harry drew an arrow on the wall, pointing up at the gap, and followed.

They seemed to have been walking for hours. Phil checked his watch. One hour, fifty four minutes and twenty five seconds to be precise. It felt much longer.

Baxter sharpened his pencil, then went back to mapping the route.

Another hour passed. Baxter's map was progressing well.

As they quietly walked down the tunnel, the sound changed. Darkness swallowed the light ahead and, at the limit of hearing, there was a double plink – a soft heartbeat – repeated over and over. Everyone was on edge, moving as quietly as they could.

The passage eventually opened into a massive gallery cavern. The walls were a honeycomb of rock pillars and tunnels leading off into the chthonian depths. Water dripped from the ceiling, *plink-plink... plink-plink*, into a deep well-like pool it had carved into the rock floor over the aeons. In the centre of the floor was a vast, ancient, ivory and grey nest built from bones. It must have been there, in use, for centuries. All kinds of skulls were scattered through it, old and new: sheep, horse, human – there was even a leopard skull.

Baxter caught his breath. 'Fuck me.'

'Told you I could find its den,' Shane stated.

'This is more of a lair,' Mabel offered.

Shane agreed.

Baxter cast his eyes over the cavern, then hefted his gun. 'It's bound to come back sooner or later. Let's get ready for it.'

Phil signalled the marksmen. They rapidly did a professional sweep of the side tunnels to make certain they were alone and safe.

On one side of the cave, a layer of different sediment looked very unstable. The walls here were definitely unsafe, with layers of sand and mud washed into the fissures between the sedimentary rock and the earlier laval, ice-cracked, stone pillars. Fallen rock and sand showed where they had eroded even further.

Phil touched a layer of sand. The light pressure dislodged it and the sand slid and dribbled away. 'This place isn't too safe.'

Tom looked worriedly at the walls and ceiling. 'This whole section is just waiting to come down.'

As the marksmen checked the tunnels, Shane, Baxter and Mabel explored the cavern. Baxter quickly sketched a plan of the natural room. If the beast had been here, it was long gone. The marksmen set up warning tripwires in the tunnels.

Shane, Mabel, Baxter and Phil made their base near the pool. Baxter pocketed the map. Meanwhile, Shane put the storm lantern on the floor. Mabel placed her gear beside Shane's and took a look around.

Baxter wanted a better view of the nest, so he opened the shutters on the storm lantern. The whole cavern was bathed in light, with shadows cast by the rocky outcrops stretching back towards the walls. He took the storm lantern over to the pile of bones.

'Won't the light scare it off?' Mabel asked, worried.

'It's not scared of people,' Shane replied. 'When it gets hungry? It'll come right to us.'

'We're the bait, then?' Her sardonic smile said it all.

Shane grinned. 'Yeah.'

The marksmen came back from rigging the alarm lines.

'Best save your torches. Let that lamp do the work,' Shane suggested.

They switched off their torches in response.

Phil indicated the nest. 'There must be a whole family of these things living here.'

Baxter frowned. 'The tracks we've seen so far only indicate one creature. Could be it's the last one left.'

Shane rubbed his cheek in thought, then blinked in acknowledgement. 'Some of these bones are virtually dust. Either this thing's several thousand years old, or...?' Shane let that thought hang.

Baxter was miffed. But he'd always been one to own up for his errors. 'That native cat scenario, I guess they were right.' *How could he have been so wrong?*

'Let's settle in,' said Phil.

Baxter finished at the nest and brought the storm lantern back over to the pool. He looked lingeringly at Mabel as he returned the lamp. He attempted to set it on the side of the pool, but it was teetering, unsafely balanced. Baxter didn't notice.

Shane did though. 'Don't leave it there!' he exclaimed.

Baxter turned to pick it up again, but the lantern slipped as he reached for it.

The gallery was plunged back into darkness. A faint light came from the pool, fading with every passing second. Deep underwater, the light showed where the lantern was still sinking. Then it cut out as water breached the casing and shorted out the electronics.

Shane switched on his head lamp and the others scrabbled to switch their torches on again. Their small beams of light scattered around the gallery where people stood, making the darkness seem more oppressive. In the blackness, light reflected on inhuman eyes. They looked from victim to victim, then vanished as The Grim moved its head and padded away.

Mabel's eyes searched the darkness, intent on her surroundings and any sign of attack. She remained utterly focussed as she backed towards Shane and her gun. When she reached him, her eyes asked, *Is it here?*

'Haven't seen it,' he affirmed.

She picked up her rifle and slung it over her shoulder. She scanned the gallery with her torch. Anger and determination held her fear in check.

'Shush!' Tom told them. Then he ordered his men, 'You lot, lock down the perimeter.'

The marksmen got into position like the well-practised, smoothly operating professionals they were. Their torch beams swept side-to-side as each one scanned the gallery for possible threats. Each man took up a position where he could guard several tunnel entrances at once.

Tom told Baxter, 'Stand there. Guard these tunnels here and here. Think you can do that?'

Baxter took umbrage at being treated like a lackey and his tone clearly said, "Fuck off, you amateur", although his response was only one word, 'Sure.'

'Keep the lady safe,' Tom told Shane.

Mabel, all attitude, didn't look like a lady who needed coddling. Shane barely responded: he was too busy checking for danger.

'Sir, those tunnels there, please,' Tom's request to Phil sounded more like a veiled order.

They waited, weapons ready.

Nothing.

More nothing.

A moment more passed.

Tom took the initiative. 'Stand down, but stay sharp. The trips will warn us if the cat comes near. Bill, Jim, get a fire going. I want some light and heat in here.'

Mabel turned to Phil to ask a question—Reflective, inhuman eyes stared at her from the darkness.

Mabel's voice died in her throat mid-word, 'Phi—'

The torch. Would it work as a weapon?

Phil turned to see what she wanted and caught her expression. 'Is it here?'

A quiet scrape of claws on rock answered his question.

'I'd say yes,' said Shane.

Mabel got her rifle ready as she nodded.

The others became instantly alert as they realised it had got past all the tripwires without setting off a single one of them. They shone their torches around, but saw no sign of the creature. The Grim had already vanished into the dark.

Away to the left came the sound of a deep, throaty, chilling laughter. Half a dozen torches aimed at the spot. But The Grim slid from sight almost before they glimpsed it: a shadow in the dark. It circled, hissing at them from the blackness.

The police marksmen were wary. The others were a good bit more than "wary"; they had already seen its handiwork. They tried to pinpoint the monster. Listening, shining their torches to try to catch a glimpse of it, of its eye-shine. But The Grim stayed always in shadow, just out of sight.

The marksmen were getting jittery. How could it avoid detection like this?

Shane, Mabel and Phil, back-to-back, protected each other as they scanned the gallery for any sign of attack.

Baxter, his back to the wall, was high on adrenaline, his every sense strained to mark the beast. Near him, Jim was cool-headed, purposeful and in "search-and-destroy" mode. It was silly, he knew, but Baxter felt safer having him there.

Baxter felt a breath of air. At the same moment,

Jim reacted to a presence. Baxter turned to face him to see why, lifting his gun to shoot at whatever might be there. In the same instant, Jim's blood splattered in an arc towards him. Baxter could see his throat was a mess, but not the attacker. Jim clutched the wound, trying to stop the arterial blood flow. Unable to cry out, he staggered backwards a few steps.

There was no sign of the beast.

Baxter saw a blur of movement, a sense of black against black, as claws ripped open Jim's chest. But Baxter couldn't see the beast itself. It moved so fast. He didn't dare shoot for fear he might hit Jim.

The others reacted to the noise. Their torches tried to find the beast, but it may as well have been invisible, a shadow in the dark, always keeping out of the light.

It made another pass, with another strike on Jim – his thigh buckled. He bled out, then crumpled and fell. The whole attack had only taken seconds. Bill grabbed the medical bag.

Shadow against shadow, they heard rather than saw as The Grim pounced on Jim and ripped him to shreds. In the background, Shane pulled out several glow sticks and cracked them into life.

There was panicked firing as the other marksmen aimed at the air around Jim. But from the moment Shane had lit the glow sticks, there was no sign of The Grim.

Baxter, in direct line of fire, stood sideways on and tried to make himself as thin as possible. All he could do was pray they missed him.

'FUCK!' he swore loudly.

Bullets impacted the wall and ceiling around him, taking out chunks of rock. A brief shower of small rocks and dust fell from the ceiling. One of the rocks struck his night-vision goggles and the lens cracked under the impact. Miraculously, Baxter was unhit but his torch wasn't so lucky. Pain flared in his hand and wrist as the bullet impact ripped the torch away. It shattered against the wall. He clutched his wrist.

'CEASE FIRE!' roared Phil.

A few more bullet hits echoed around the cavern as the panic-fire stopped. But it was too much for the over-stressed geology. The fragile wall started to give; the ceiling above Baxter crumbled.

It was a cave-in!

Baxter ran clear, down the nearest tunnel, as choking dust enveloped everything.

Shane, Mabel, Phil and the marksmen jumped clear of the gravel and rocks that tumbled down. They coughed and spluttered as the clouds of fine powdered rock got into their lungs.

Slowly, the dust cleared.

Their torches and glow sticks revealed a wall of rubble, that blocked off almost a quarter of the exit tunnels where the ceiling had collapsed.

There was no sign of Baxter.

Dave lay unconscious, part-buried by rubble.

Pitch black.

The noise of rivulets of falling gravel and sand finally stopped.

There was a long moment of silence while Baxter found his bearings and recovered from the shock of nearly being totally buried. He realised that he was still breathing, still alive. And he couldn't see, because there was no light to see by. His attempts to move were accompanied by the sound of falling rubble as he freed himself from the debris. He felt bruised all over.

'Ow! Fuck,' Baxter swore.

There was the sound of more movement as he stood and freed himself fully.

Further down the tunnel, a rock dislodged, as if stepped on.

Baxter froze. The only sound in the dark was his breathing – it was all he could hear. He swallowed, then held his breath, listening. There were no other noises, so he started breathing again, as quietly as he could.

A horrible bubbling laugh echoed down the passage ahead of him.

In the gallery cave, Shane and the others warily placed all their glow sticks around the floor of the cavern.

The light revealed no sign of The Grim.

Relieved and secure, Phil and the marksmen moved to help Dave, while Mabel walked to the rubble wall which used to be the tunnel Baxter had run down. Shane followed her.

'Baxter!' she called, hopefully. She listened. There was no reply. 'Are you okay?' she shouted again, then, 'Baxter!'

He was too much of a pain in the arse to be gone; she knew he'd turn up again like the rotten rat he was. He wasn't dead. Couldn't be.

Shane touched her arm. 'He'll be fine. He's a survivor.'

'Yeah.'

Beside Dave's prone form, Tom smiled and in the same moment Bill said with relief, 'There's a pulse. He's still alive.'

He and the others started pulling the rubble off

their comrade, while Phil stood guard, keeping watch for the beast.

It was still pitch black in the tunnel. There was the rustle of cloth as Baxter opened his rucksack by touch. Suddenly the tunnel was bathed in light revealing he stood at a 'Y' intersection. He clutched the glow stick he'd just cracked into life—

—And registered a mouth full of fangs coming right at him.

'OH FUCK!' he yelled, as he brought up his arm to block the attack; simultaneously he turned and legged it. In that same moment The Grim fled from the light.

Baxter sprinted down the narrow tunnel. He careered off the walls at each turn, but somehow he kept his feet. Eventually it hit him; he was not dead yet. *Why not?* He looked back.

There was nothing there, no sign of the monster. And it had been a monster. Cat-like, but certainly not a cat of any kind that he knew. He even had the brief impression that there may have been wings, momentarily glimpsed – but maybe that was just an illusion created by his subconscious mind, because of Mabel's previous assertion?

Stumbling to a ragged halt, he leaned back against the wall, sucking in air. After a moment he lifted his hand and looked at the glow stick.

'Not feline,' he said raggedly between breaths.

He pulled out his night-vision goggles and checked them, but they were bust, useless, cracked where the stone smashed into them. He dropped them at the side of the tunnel.

Dave leaned against the wall, conscious but woozy

and in pain, his leg very obviously broken.

Bill finished tying the last knot on the splint. 'Keep still if you can,' he told Dave.

As the others stood guard, Phil apprised them of the situation. 'Bad news is, Baxter has the map.'

'And the spare glow sticks,' Shane added.

Phil pointed at the rubble. 'Worse news, that used to be the way out. The only way out.'

Shane smiled.

'Good news is, I got a good look at the map of the mine, memorised it. And if Baxter's mapping skills are as accurate as they appeared, a big section of the mine isn't far from here. One of the tunnels was blocked off because it joined a dangerous natural cave system. We've already passed several side tunnels, so there's probably another way back that will take us to the mine.' Shane grabbed a bone and sketched what he remembered on the ground.

The others each took it in turn to crane over and see.

Shane pointed at a mine tunnel that ran near the gallery.

'This is the tunnel we're looking for. It joins with others that lead to the exit tunnel. *If* we can find it.'

Phil sounded confident. 'This maze is like a honeycomb, everything joins to everything else. We just need to head in the right direction.'

'Let's hope,' agreed Shane, voicing the nagging paranoid doubt they all felt.

A rock fell. The clatter made them all jump.

Baxter set off down the narrow tunnel holding the glow stick ahead of him. He broke into a jog and rapidly came to an intersection. He could see that several passages came off this larger one, which sloped downwards slightly. He looked up the other way. More tunnels led off into the subterranean black.

Baxter pulled out the map and stuffed several more unused glow sticks into his breast pocket. Then he started to sketch the way he'd just come.

There was a faint slithering sound in the dark behind him. Baxter's head shot up like a gazelle sensing a predator. He brought the glow stick around, but he could see no sign of the beast. He realised he didn't expect to. This thing was far too quick on its feet for that.

Echoing from a side corridor farther up the slope, deep, inhuman laughter confirmed what he knew; it was there, waiting for its moment.

Baxter swivelled the glow stick and caught the barest glimpse of something dark against the grey rock. From the deepest shadow, there came a long, menacing hiss.

'It hates the light.' *Shane had been right*, he thought ruefully. He guessed he owed both Shane and Mabel an apology.

He quickly checked the map, then deftly sketched what he could see. There were no clues in the topography as to which was the way to go. And the glow stick was fading. He had lots, but eventually he would run out.

He chose a random tunnel that might go towards the mine and ran down it.

The chuckle was right behind him!

Baxter cracked a spare glow stick and dropped it at his feet. He heard the hiss and angry screech from the beast. It had been virtually on top of him!

In the gallery cavern, the glow sticks were starting to fade. Instinctively the group moved closer together.

'We need to get Dave to a hospital,' Tom said. 'We can come back later with the right equipment to deal with this thing.'

Bill and Harry laced their fingers together and cradled their arms to make a seat for Dave. Almost unnoticed, Dave's torch died as the battery ran out. Once he was comfortably sitting between them, the group set out nervously.

The tunnel they went down started out well enough with solid rock walls, but they quickly discovered seams of the collapsible sandstone running across it.

Mabel touched the wall and a hand-sized chunk of rock melted under her palm. Sand dribbled away. In the background, Bill's torch failed.

'Should we go this way?' Mabel asked, concerned by the fragility of the walls.

'It's the most likely tunnel to get us back to the mine,' Shane replied.

'No one touch the walls,' Phil requested needlessly. They were all aware of the danger of further cave-ins.

They walked in single file along the centre of the tunnel. Bill and Harry shuffled crabwise down the narrow, twisting tunnel as they cradled Dave between them.

Baxter had walked a long way and was sure he must be nearing the mine by now, if his sense of direction hadn't failed him. He was fully aware of how tricky it could be above ground, never mind under the surface, where the natural tunnels twisted and turned, running wherever the water that carved them had chosen to flow.

Baxter saw a fissure in the wall and knew he had to see what, if anything, it might lead to. He pushed the glow stick through the gap and smiled when he saw that there was an empty space, a corridor, on the other side.

He squeezed carefully through, between the solid stone faces, trying not to get stuck; praying that he wouldn't be attacked while he was jammed between the rough limestone slabs, as he wriggled sideways, into a man-made tunnel.

Baxter paused to catch his breath on the other side of the fissure. He held up the glow stick to get a better look at his surroundings. The light revealed power and air ducts running at shoulder height along the walls. They were a welcome sight and a real relief.

He checked the map again. The fissure was unmarked. He rechecked the position and then marked it on the map. He knew where he was now.

Phil and the others moved cautiously down the twisting sandstone tunnel. Each accidental touch sent rivulets of sand and small rocks cascading down the walls. The tunnel appeared to be on the verge of collapse. They turned a corner and saw an ancient wooden wall completely barricading the passage.

'This is it!' exclaimed Tom excitedly.

He reached out and grabbed a section of the barricade and started pulling.

'Wait!' commanded Phil.

Tom paused.

'He's right,' said Shane. 'When this gives, it's going to make a racket and that damned monster'll be on us quick as a brer down its hole. Best we all break it together. Keep the noise in one short burst.'

Harry and Bill carefully lowered Dave to the floor and joined the others at the barricade.

They used their rifles as levers, grasping the planking wherever there was a handhold. On a silent countdown they all heaved together. The ancient wood protested, then splintered and cracked, large chunks of it coming away under the assault, to reveal a hole large enough to get through. They smiled in silent celebration. Mabel hugged Phil and Shane.

Phil addressed the group, 'We need to be as quiet as possible now. I don't want us to be an easy lunch.'

They all agreed with that.

They quickly made their way into the connecting mine tunnel. As they went, Harry's torch failed. Mabel hung back to light their way. The new passage had been carved by hand through the rock, a long time in the past. Chisel marks were clear on the uneven walls which twisted up and down, this way and that, as it followed a quartz seam.

Phil led, followed by Shane and Mabel. Bill and Harry, carrying Dave, were next. Tom followed at the back, guarding the rear.

Phil's torch failed. Shane removed the mounted torch from his helmet and gave the unit to Phil so that he could still light the way.

The tunnel narrowed. Bill and Harry had to scoot through sideways again. Dave's foot touched the stone wall. He cried out in agony and clamped his hand over his mouth to mute it.

'Sorry,' Harry whispered.

'It's okay. It's only pain,' Dave whispered back.

The others looked over, checking on him. Dave jiggled his head to indicate, apologetically, that he was fine.

The torch unit Phil now carried and Tom's torch died within seconds of each other. The team prepared to switch over to the night-vision goggles. Mabel's torch sputtered and died. Shane helped her with her goggles, then checked them. She gave a thumbs up to indicate they were on and working.

Now that it was dark, Mabel was as twitchy as a stoat. Shane put his hand on her shoulder and smiled comfortingly. Her answering smile wavered a bit.

They moved off again.

They were approaching a crossroads. Shane indicated that they should keep going on this tunnel.

As they passed the crossroads, the shadows in the cross passage came to life. Clawed hands stabbed into Dave's back, driving the breath out of him. His exhaled mist of frothy blood spattered his friends. He was abruptly hauled free and dragged back into the darkness.

The marksmen tried to find a target, but there was no sign of The Grim or their compatriot. He was gone. Vanished.

Baxter held the glow stick above him as he walked. Keeping the tunnel well-lit, he checked constantly for signs of danger. He seemed safe enough. He approached a wide sloping side tunnel that lead up to a higher level. Baxter paused, listening. There were no sounds of any kind from up there.

He quietly sidled to the opposite side of the passage and peered in. He was relieved to see there was nothing there but darkness and rock. He crept past it, keeping a wary eye open for any sign of movement. But there was none. Baxter kept walking.

He followed the tunnel around a narrow hairpin bend. Once he passed this, the passage opened out and ran straight. Up ahead, he could make out the entrance to a room. Air and power ducts went into it. On the wall by the door, covered by glass, hung a mildewed map of the mine and its levels. But between Baxter and the room, there were the scant remains of what used to be a ladder on the wall. A dark patch on the ceiling marked where the egress point to the next level was.

With great trepidation, Baxter approached the hole in the roof. He hoped the beast was behind him, but he couldn't be certain. It knew these tunnels and it could be anywhere. Warily he looked up into the hole. It was, as expected, another access to the tunnel on the level above. Baxter skipped hurriedly past the opening and went on towards the room.

He reached the door and pushed the glow stick through, to reveal a familiar small room with ancient broken junk scattered across the floor. The severed ends of the twin sets of air and power ducts gaped open, uselessly. Baxter nearly laughed with relief. He cracked a new glow stick and chucked it into the middle of the floor. Then he turned back to the tunnel and made for the slope up to the next level.

The group pounded down the chiselled tunnel at speed in a defensive formation, weapons at the ready. Phil was on point, then Shane, Mabel, Bill and Harry, with Tom bringing up the rear.

Baxter unpacked the brick-sized package and carefully unwrapped it. It contained two narrow blocks of C4 explosive with detonators and a radio control. He cut off precisely the amount of explosive he wanted from one of them and packed that into the ceiling above the sloping side tunnel. The rest of the C4 got rewrapped and stored back in the package.

Ahead, a T-junction crossed the chiselled tunnel. The new tunnel looked clear. The group barely slowed as they entered it. Power and air ducts ran at shoulder height along its length. Phil let out a yell and vanished from sight!

The others, alarmed, stopped, almost falling over themselves in their haste – they quickly realised what happened. Phil had tripped and was sprawled on the ground. Shane only just managed to avoid stepping on Dave's corpse.

The group milled about for a second, then the marksmen's professionalism took control again.

Shane helped Phil to his feet. Bill checked Dave's pulse, despite it being obvious the man was dead. Mabel noticed a blur of deep shadow in the darkness as The Grim hurtled out of the hewn tunnel, bowling Bill over. They rolled, locked together by The Grim's claws and teeth, until they smacked up against the wall.

The Grim released its hold on Bill's neck. It noticed Mabel staring at it. She took an involuntary step backwards. It locked eyes with her and smiled. Mabel shuddered and gave a small squeak, then realised she was holding a gun. The Grim padded towards her. She didn't bother to aim. From waist height she just pointed and fired.

The bullet slammed into The Grim. She pulled the trigger again and again. Then *click*, the chamber was empty. Mabel's eyes widened with fear.

The Grim looked cross. It launched itself at her. She stepped sideways as she shrank back from its fury. Phil hurled himself between them, bringing his rifle up to use as a club, and took the full force of the attack.

'PHIL!' Mabel screamed.

The others, avoiding both her and Phil, aimed carefully and fired at the monster. Meanwhile, Mabel retreated and reloaded her gun.

The Grim ignored the bullet hits as it fed on Phil. The wounds closed up as soon as they were made.

Shane couldn't believe what he was seeing. 'It's healing itself!' he exclaimed, outraged.

The Grim finished with Phil and started to come after them.

The marksmen were unnerved by the beast's refusal to die. Shane gritted his teeth and kept firing while the others reloaded in turns. Each wound healed, but it was taking longer every time.

'It killed Phil,' Mabel said in a small voice filled with despair and regret.

They retreated. Mabel, her anger taking over, walked backwards calmly and shot it in the chest. The wound only half-healed.

A malicious thought struck Mabel. She grabbed her pouch of salt and purposefully broke the drawstring as she pulled it from her belt. She hurled it at the wound. On target. Salt went everywhere. And everywhere it landed on The Grim, it wounded it further.

That hurt! The Grim looked at the damage, then looked at her.

Mabel smiled.

It leapt over the spilled salt and started after her. Mabel emptied her gun into it, then started reloading.

The Grim snarled and kept coming. Slow, steady, purposeful – invoking fear in the men watching.

Tom fired, then reloaded when the chamber was finished and started firing again.

Despite the wounds, The Grim seemed mostly unaffected, although it was definitely angry.

'The bullets aren't working!' called Tom.

'The salt! Use the salt!' Mabel shouted back.

Those who had salt pouches and were close enough, hurled them at the monster.

The Grim screeched and hissed and gave them a murderous look.

'I think we've pissed it off,' yelled Shane.

Mabel checked the ground behind her as she retreated and spotted Baxter at the turn in the tunnel.

Baxter motioned, *Come here!*

'Get over here! Hurry up!' he shouted.

Shane and the others snatched a look back.

'Come on!' Baxter yelled at them.

They sped up their retreat. The Grim looked at its injuries, then hissed angrily. Harry, terrified, emptied his chamber into it. The Grim changed pace; speeding up, it loped after them. Mabel paused to shoot again. Shane grabbed her and pulled her away. They caught up to the others.

 The group approached the sloping side tunnel, ran past it. The Grim approached the opening and started to pass—

Baxter hit the radio control detonator switch and a massive explosion took out the roof at the entrance to the sloping tunnel.

—The Grim reacted to the noise, as a tonne of granite fell on top of it.

Cautiously, the team returned to the heap of stone to look at where the beast had been. Baxter followed and prodded the rubble with a toe. He'd definitely got it!

They all relaxed and began to celebrate.

A thought struck Tom and he said, 'You brought explosives?'

'I thought that if I didn't kill it, we could always seal it in. Problem solved,' said Baxter. He smiled at Shane. 'Better than a net.'

Shane ignored the dig.

Tom levelled a look at Baxter. 'I may have to arrest you later.'

'I have a licence,' Baxter confirmed. He looked at the large heap of rubble. 'I got you, you son of a bitch.'

There was a sudden grinding noise as stone shifted. The debris started moving.

'You've got to be kidding!' exclaimed Tom.

'Run!' shouted Shane.

They all sprinted down the tunnel, cleared the bend and made for the small room that marked the exit passages.

Rocks heaved upwards and tumbled away. The Grim rose out of the debris and hauled itself clear. It shook itself, scattering chips of rock and dust from its fur. Then it dashed along the corridor after them with terrifying speed.

The survivors sprinted through the room and took the tagged exit tunnel. A moment later, The Grim darted through and bounded after them. As it hurtled in pursuit Baxter, without breaking stride, turned and shot. He hit the beast solidly, but it was still coming and gaining on them fast.

The Grim changed angle. It was after Mabel!

Mabel checked behind her and, in the same moment it leaped, she tripped over a stone and fell flat on her face. The Grim sailed over her body and landed squarely on Tom's shoulders, knocking him to the ground. It recovered, snarled, and looked back.

Mabel was hauling herself to her feet. She locked eyes with it.

Tom tried to heave it off. The Grim looked down at him. It changed its position and flipped him over so that they were face-to-face. Tom fumbled for his handgun, found it, and fired at point blank range. The creature clasped Tom's gun and hand in its clawed fingers and broke his wrist. Tom screamed. Without effort, the beast ripped his hand off, and chucked both it and the gun away.

Tom was still screaming when it lunged for his throat.

Mabel slipped passed them. She wanted to help, but it was too late for that. The Grim was drinking its fill of Tom's blood and he was definitely dead. She ran for the exit while it fed.

The Grim used Tom's blood to fuel its healing process and, by the time it had finished feeding, it was almost fully healed.

If The Grim had looked up from its gruesome feast, it would have seen that the silhouettes of its prey showed clearly in the entrance as they escaped from the mine. The grey of early dawn tinted the sky. Storm clouds lined the horizon.

The survivors raced down the slope. The faint light

showed the break in the trees where the path lead back to their vehicles. They plunged along the footpath and broke from the trees onto the hard gravel surface of the turning circle.

The Grim stood outside the entrance to the cave, raised its head and let out a bloodcurdling cry. Then it unfurled its wings and launched itself into the air.

Its cry echoed across the mountainside as Baxter, Mabel, Shane and Harry ran to their vehicles.

Harry started to reach into his pocket— then remembered it was a work vehicle and he didn't have the keys. He rushed to the Humvee where Baxter was struggling to get the lock to work.

Baxter swore as he realised that the keys needed a new battery. He grimaced at himself, glad that everyone was too busy to notice, and resorted to opening it manually.

A moment later, Harry arrived at the Humvee looking for help.

'Need a ride?' Baxter asked cheerfully.

Finally he managed to unlock the Humvee, got in and reached across with one hand to open the passenger door for Harry, keying the ignition with the other.

Shane and Mabel got to the Land Rover. She habitually left it unlocked, so it only took a moment to get in and start the engine. They accelerated toward the exit track.

A tree trunk smacked into the ground across the track, blocking the way. Mabel slammed on the brakes.

The Grim landed by the tree trunk, chuckling.

Baxter saw what was happening and turned the Humvee. An old, narrow track full of brambles and seedlings beckoned. He raced towards it.

Mabel crunched into reverse and accelerated backwards. She spotted Baxter, sprayed gravel in a handbrake turn, steered into the skid and followed.

Both vehicles were tossed about as they raced down the overgrown farm track.

Shane indicated dead ahead and said calmly, 'You know what's down there.'

'Yep,' Mabel replied. 'But I'm not going that way. I'm going *that* way!' She pointed to a bridlepath that crossed their track. 'You better warn him,' she said.

Shane grabbed the radio. 'Baxter! Turn left! Turn left!'

In the Humvee, Baxter heard him loud and clear. He looked at the only turning left, a pony track through virtually impassable terrain. He flicked off the radio.

'So, I get hung up and it can eat me while you make your escape?' he asked himself, cynically.

Harry was shocked by the callousness of this. 'The bastards!' he exclaimed.

Shane and Mabel saw the Humvee speed down the track, ignoring the turn off.

Shane shouted into the radio, 'That's the mire!'

He realised he was only getting static.

Baxter reached back and gave them the finger.

Mabel steered the Land Rover onto the bridlepath. It was difficult going. The vehicle was forced to slow down, but Mabel piled on as much speed as they could muster. They needed to get over the exceedingly rough, uphill terrain. They got rattled and bumped to bits, but they were still going.

'They won't get far,' Shane stated. 'Rumour is, the army lost an entire tank in there once.'

Mabel slammed on the brakes. 'We should go back for them,' she said.

At first, the Humvee made good headway over lush green grass, then became waterlogged in the mire. Water sluiced up on either side as it spun its wheels in mud up to its axles.

Mabel crunched into reverse, as the engine protested. She finally found the gear and started going back. In the rear view mirror, she saw The Grim as it bounded past.

Realising it was too late, she stopped the Land Rover. Shane reached for one rifle. Mabel grabbed the other.

Baxter tried to rock the Humvee loose. Forward, backwards, forward, backwards. He knew the ground was too wet and he was just digging the vehicle in deeper, so he stopped. He didn't like the idea, but he could use the footwell mats under the drive tyres to give them purchase.

He'd just have to wash them afterwards, or buy new ones.

Harry saw The Grim in the rear view mirror.

The creature reached the Humvee; Harry locked the doors as it thudded onto the bonnet.

Baxter looked up.

At the Land Rover, Shane aimed at The Grim and started firing. Mabel joined him.

On the bonnet of the Humvee, The Grim ignored the bullet hits that smacked into it from the side. They healed instantly.

Harry pulled out his sidearm.

The Grim reached forward, stabbed its front claws into the windscreen, grabbed the frame and pulled the whole section out of the vehicle. Then, it casually tossed the glass panel aside.

Harry was acutely aware that, with the windscreen glass gone, all the creature had to do was reach in. He barely had to aim it was so close. He shot The Grim, hitting it squarely every time, as he emptied his revolver into it. Chest. Neck. Head. The wounds healed instantly.

The Grim hissed.

While Harry was busy shooting the beast, Baxter unlocked his door and cracked it open.

The Grim spotted him trying to leave. It locked eyes with him.

Baxter, terrified, grabbed Harry and bodily pulled the man between himself and The Grim.

Harry yelled as Baxter hauled him across. He tried to defend himself. Still shooting with one hand, and hitting at The Grim in vain with the other, as the creature struck.

Harry's body bucked and twitched as The Grim ripped into him and started to feed.

Mabel ran out of ammunition. Shane handed her some more bullets; he was running low too.

Baxter snatched his rifle, leaned against the door and fell out of the vehicle as he tried to roll clear. He picked himself up and sploshed away through the bog as fast as he could. Mud sucked at his walking boots with each step and he quickly ended up as mired as the Humvee.

The Grim finished with Harry. It ignored the continuing rain of bullets that Mabel and Shane peppered into it. Instead, it focused on Baxter. When it saw his predicament, the beast chuckled and began its stalk.

Baxter, stuck fast, heard The Grim's mirth and saw it approaching. How the heck could he get out of this? He couldn't turn around to get a proper shot. Then he remembered an obvious option. He grabbed his belt knife, reached down into the mud and, with several cuts, he severed the laces of one boot. His foot came free. A small victory. But The Grim was closing in on him.

He bent his knee and awkwardly half-turned, carefully repositioning his free foot. He unslung his rifle and aimed. The perfect headshot through the right eye. *Click!*

Preternaturally calm, he smoothly loaded two shells into the chamber. He aimed again, shot The Grim in the eye, then shot again. It blinked and turned its head just in time. His attempts to exploit its weak spot just made the beast extra mean.

It grabbed the rifle and pulled it out of Baxter's hands.

Baxter's free foot stepped backwards, leaving his sock behind in the sucking marsh. He drew his knife crosswise, face-height, in high dudgeon.

The Grim looked at the blade, then looked into

Baxter's eyes and smiled. It lifted its hand and vicious claws snicked, one by one, into view.

Baxter knew he was as good as dead, but there was no way he was giving in.

The Grim slashed at him. Baxter defended with the knife. Claws sheared through the metal as if it wasn't there. Sections of blade flew off into the mud. Baxter looked at the useless stub. He hurled it and it smacked satisfyingly into The Grim's nose, bouncing off. The Grim shook off the pain, snarled and pounced straight for his throat.

Mabel and Shane watched helplessly from their posts by the Land Rover.

'How do we stop this thing?' she asked at a loss, not expecting him to know.

Shane reloaded his gun. He only had three shells left.

'Lets get out of here,' he said, opening the door. They clambered back inside.

Mabel put the Land Rover in gear and jammed her foot on the accelerator. The vehicle bit into the rough terrain and hauled them up the rise.

The Grim watched them leaving and dropped Baxter's corpse. It started after them.

Shane swallowed. 'It's coming,' he said.

Mabel stopped the Land Rover and turned to Shane. 'We can't outrun it. This is where we make our stand.'

She got out, then reached back in and grabbed her gun.

Shane knew they were out of options. *May as well*

get on with it. He got out too.

'Sometimes, I get a call and I really wish I hadn't answered the phone. You ever get that?' he asked wryly.

'Now and again,' she said and chuckled darkly.

The Grim darted towards them. It was nearly on them.

Shane aimed carefully and fired all his remaining shells. He hit The Grim squarely. Mabel aimed and shot once, then *click*. She tried again. *Click*. She was out of ammo too.

The Grim was coming right at her. Mabel changed her grip and used the gun as a club.

The Grim slapped it away. The force of the blow sent the rifle spinning back. It cracked into the side of the Land Rover, denting the door and breaking the rifle's stock.

Shane grabbed the colourful plastic gun hanging from his belt as a last, desperate measure. He knew it wouldn't do anything; it was only water. But he pulled up the water pistol and fired anyway.

The Grim shrieked in pain.

Shane squirted the beast again.

Steam rose from the monster, as the holy water ate into its flesh. It was furious. Mabel forgotten, Shane had its full attention now.

The water pistol was empty. Shane grabbed his last bag of salt and hurled it at The Grim as it attacked, snarling.

'Bollocks,' said Shane. Then it was on him. He was knocked to the ground.

The Grim pinned his arms and revealed its fangs to him.

'I hope you choke!'

The Grim savaged Shane's face, then went for his neck, the blood healing its steaming wounds.

All the while, Mabel tried to get it off Shane. It completely ignored her and her efforts. She hit it, then kicked it, then finally grabbed its tail and pulled.

The Grim looked around and hissed. Shane was too weak to do anything. He was losing consciousness.

Mabel realised what she was doing and dropped its tail. She looked for a weapon. Her broken rifle was the only thing nearby.

The Grim held Shane down with one hand. With the other, it snagged her foot, tripping her. As Mabel went down, she grabbed the barrel of the gun. The Grim smiled and pulled her towards it.

She used the gun like a club and smacked The Grim hard across the nose with the wooden end. Another section of wood splintered off, leaving the butt sharp and pointy.

The Grim spat its fury. It reached out its hand and grabbed her by the throat, lifting her effortlessly from the ground. As she choked, The Grim turned back to Shane and finally went for the kill. Only then did it turn back to deal with Mabel.

Unable to breathe, turning blue, she mustered the last of her strength and stabbed The Grim in the heart with the broken butt of the rifle.

The creature stopped, the breath knocked from it. It dropped her and reeled back, gurgling. The beast stumbled backwards, pawing at the gun. It tripped and sat down heavily, then fell to its side. It got a grip on the gun, then lay prone, gasping, trying to heal the wound.

Mabel couldn't believe it. Was it really dying?

The Grim rallied, pulling the splintered gun from its chest. Breath rasping, angry as hell.

It stood up.

Mabel stumbled back, away from it.

The Grim started towards her, but stopped. She was silhouetted by the pink glow of sunrise. The storm clouds on the horizon were parting. Pink, red and gold fringed their edges.

Light hit The Grim and its skin blistered. It hissed and leaped away, then fled back up Crag Tor, heading for its cave.

Mabel stood on the moor, feeling numb, lost, alone.

After a moment, she went to Shane's corpse and knelt down beside him, touching his wounds, his face, willing him to be alive.

In Mabel's office, a young policeman, P.C. Joseph Collins, looked on helplessly as Mabel grabbed a few things and added them to her luggage.

On her desk, "The Parks Warden" magazine lay open at the careers section. Several jobs were circled in blue ink.

P.C. Collins was barely out of the Police Training Centre and didn't know how to deal with this civilian's refusal to cooperate. She was a material witness, but he knew he couldn't force her to stay and help.

'You can't go,' Joseph pleaded.

Mabel finished packing and grabbed her bags. 'I'm outta here.'

She left the office, with P.C. Collins trailing behind her.

In the town square, she went straight to her Land Rover and slung her bags into it. She looked over her shoulder at the young policeman.

'The beast is nocturnal because its skin is photo-reactive. Light damages it. Bet it really hates the sun! Make sure everyone stays indoors at night.'

'Please don't go? We need you!'

Mabel got in and started the engine.

'You're a witness!'

'You've had my statement. Call me when it comes to court.'

Mabel drove off, accelerating as she went.

She had made good time up the M73 and had decided to pause for an early evening cup of coffee to revitalise herself for the rest of the trip. A fast walk around the car park, then a short stop in the shop and she was quickly back on the road. Mabel drank her coffee from a service station cup as she drove, listening to the radio.

A sign up ahead proclaimed "SCOTLAND WELCOMES YOU". She hoped it was accurate, as she planned to spend the next several years, maybe longer, working here. Mabel smiled hopefully at the sign as she crossed the border.

The Scottish mountain sunlight gave a warm, yet high altitude, wintry-fresh feel to both the air and the landscape. It reminded her of the two-week holiday in Norway that her parents had sent her on. She'd loved every moment of it.

The Braemar Park warden's cottage looked perfect. She instinctively knew it was a place she could relax and sleep well in. Mabel's Land Rover stood a short distance away, where she'd parked it, just off the gravel covered road.

The outgoing Park Warden, Angus, was already approaching. He looked to be in his early fifties, but he was much older. He was retiring, which was why the vacancy had opened up. He had a reddish hint to his curly blond hair, while white peppered his beard and moustaches.

Mabel liked him instantly. He had a firm handshake and a gentle quietness about him that was common to people who worked with and around wildlife.

When he spoke, he had a deep melodic voice.

'The Cairngorms are wonderful. You're going to love it here.'

Her smile widened. 'I already do.'

'I've left you a little welcome gift in the corner cupboard. Help you christen the place.'

'Thank you, Angus, you're very kind.'

Angus handed her the keys to the cottage. 'There you go. You take care now.'

'You, too.'

As Angus headed off, Mabel moved her gear from the Land Rover to the cottage.

She turned in the doorway and looked out at the scenery. It was stunning. Very different from the views she was used to on Dartmoor. It had more in common with the views from Holmenkollen, or the ski lift near Bergen, which looked out over the Norwegian countryside.

Mabel wanted to see what the view was like at night and, more importantly, she needed to test her nerve. Could she still go out in the dark after what she had been through?

Two and a half weeks later, she already felt as though she'd been in Braemar for months. She had taken to the area and the people like a duck to water.

Mabel was at the local pub, The Change-Hoose, where she had joined the locals to enjoy a pint or two. The television played the news in the background.

The locals had taken to Mabel right away. She sat at a table with her new Scottish friends: Hamish, a man around her own age, the much younger MacDougal, who was barely in his twenties and Tod, an older man in his late fifties, who reminded her of Shane, with his mischievous sense of humour. He was also a bit of a bard. He had the gift of the gab and the ability to hold a room enthralled with his stories.

They had taken over one of the tables tucked away at the side of the main room. There they talked, listened, drank and had a jolly good time joking about things that had happened to them at work in their various different jobs.

On the television, Honey Ripley covered one of the main story updates.

'After twenty-one days of carnage, the Dartmoor Beast finally seems to have stopped its reign of terror. It has been five days since the last attack and there is no sign of the beast. One local resident claims to have shot and killed the monster.'

MacDougal laughed, then said, 'Daft southern softies, letting a lion escape. What do they expect!'

Hamish looked at Mabel.

'You're from down there...?' Hamish asked.

Mabel took a deep draught from her pint,

considered a moment, then said, 'Why d'ya think I came here?'

Tod put down his drink and said, in the tone of voice which meant he was going to regale them with one of his tales, 'Reminds me of the story of The Boggle.'

He paused while his friends laughed.

'Ach! You and your tall stories!' MacDougal scoffed teasingly.

As Tod resumed speaking, they settled down to listen to his tale. 'Grandma told me this one.'

Mabel choked on her pint.

Black Alice, book one – The White Gate

Alice was tired. The eight-year-old girl stood at the work bench in the healing room at the front of the house.

While she crushed herbs with the pestle and mortar, she concentrated, blocking out the sensations in the room behind her: the sickness and fevered ramblings, the fear, the feelings of loss and its associated emotions of pain and anger.

It had only been a few weeks, but it felt as though her life had always been like this. Rationally, she knew things would change, would get better, return to normal.

She concentrated at a deeper level, made contact with the healing earth, and brought a thread of life-giving energy up from the ground to gently surround and rejuvenate her mother. Alice hoped that Maylin didn't detect this new, more subtle attempt to help and misread it again as dangerous to them both. It wasn't. Her mother followed the traditional method and didn't believe there was another way. Her mother couldn't *see* what Alice *saw*. Alice *knew* her mother was wrong; Alice could *see* her dying a little with each intervention and, currently, with not enough time to recover her life-force fully between each treatment.

Behind her, Maylin, looking exhausted, bent over yet another person who was recovering from plague under her careful ministration.

Golden healing energy welled out from the centre of Maylin's body to fill her aura, then she poured it into her patient, replacing their aura's blotchy-grey sickness with this healing light of her own life-force. The patient stirred and Maylin moved on to the next cot and the next patient, one of many occupied cots that crowded the room.

As far as she knew, Maylin was the only healer in Hapstead, the only healer in the region. And her work kept her very busy, especially now.

A dozen fresh graves marked the edge of the cemetery where a burial service for Emily Cooper, the wife of the Mayor, was just finishing. The group who were gathered to mourn looked to Mayor Cooper, their leader, as he talked to them passionately – and they appeared more like a lynch mob with every word. 'Follow me and we'll rid our village of this curse!' he shouted. The mourners cheered in response.

On the village streets, the people were more concerned with either tending to the sick or keeping themselves to themselves, than getting on with their daily lives. Working to earn a living no longer seemed such a priority.

A wife and daughter supported their man as they carried him towards a hut. Inside, Maylin welcomed the newcomers, black rings under her eyes testifying to the added exhaustion of her latest round of healing. She indicated that they should help the man onto the cot in front of her. Once he was comfortable, Maylin stepped forward. She closed her eyes again, centred herself, and a moment later the golden glow of healing energy surrounded her. She fed it through her hands into the man until he too was glowing. When she had finished, he was in a natural sleep and the signs of plague had almost left him. Maylin, utterly spent, leaned for a moment against the cot, then pulled herself upright and smiled at the woman and girl as they thanked her.

There was a commotion outside. The door burst open as a small mob, led by Mayor Cooper, pushed into the hut, closely followed by Randolph the blacksmith.

'You brought this plague on us, witch!' snarled the Mayor. 'My wife is dead at your hands. They're all dead because of you!'

'No,–' Maylin tried to protest.

But the mob wasn't listening. They grabbed her and pulled her from the hut.

'Mother!' Alice shouted in terror. She felt as though she was watching a terrible, time-clouded memory unfold all over again.

As Mayor Cooper followed them out, he looked back at Randolph and pointed to Alice. 'Bring the brat, too!' he spat.

The blacksmith looked at the frightened girl, hardened his resolve, then seized Alice by the arm and dragged her out to join the others. It was only fitting that the witch's daughter should be punished by the mob for her part in helping her mother raise the black magics that had brought the plague.

A pyre had been built at the northern edge of Hapstead. Maylin and Alice were dragged over to it by the mob, who ignored Maylin's screams of protest. More than half the village had turned out to cheer on the witch hunters.

Trapped in Randolph's firm grip, Alice was

helpless. She silently took it all in with big, frightened eyes. Instinctively, she felt she didn't want to remember, or live through, what happened next.

As Maylin was pulled onto the pyre, she shot a pleading look towards the blacksmith.

'Please don't hurt my daughter. She's done nothing wrong; she's only a child.'

Maylin was lashed to the stake, then fires were set amongst the bone-dry kindling, rapidly turning the piled wood under her into an inferno.

'No!' screamed Alice, trying to break free of Randolph's hold and run to help her mother, but the young girl was no match for his strength. She tried to turn away from the sight, but Mayor Cooper grabbed her hair and forced her to watch her mother's death throes. Randolph looked down at the helpless girl; she had stopped struggling in his grip.

The baying and jeers from the crowd faded to silence. Alice could take in nothing but the horror of the scene in front of her.